LONGSWORD

Longsword,
Earl of Salisbury

by

Thomas Leland

Edited and Introduced
by Albert Power

Swan River Press
Dublin, Ireland
MMXXII

Longsword
by Thomas Leland

Published by
Swan River Press
Dublin, Ireland
in February MMXXII

www.swanriverpress.ie
brian@swanriverpress.ie

This edition © Swan River Press
Introduction © Albert Power

Cover design by Meggan Kehrli from
"Never Let Go" © Ellen McDermott

Set in Garamond by Steve J. Shaw

Paperback Edition
ISBN 978-1-78380-757-4

Swan River Press published
a limited hardback edition of
Longsword in July 2012.

Contents

Introduction

*L*ongsword, *Earl of Salisbury* is a psychological tragedy of the olden time decked with stirring scenes of high drama and excitement. At one level it is a tale about the rot of mistrust, which once introduced into relations between spouses, brings a burden of anguish nigh impossible to ease. At another it is a morality fable on the depth of degradation to which the lure of lust and ambition can drag one. Played out from its first page to its last at an unrelenting romp, and freighted in places with the heavy hand of menace, *Longsword* is in all respects a Gothic novel of true hue—replete with thrilling scenes of abduction, assault on womanly virtue, monastic machination, shipwreck, piratical attack, jousts and sword-play. In one respect alone the list of incidentals is lacking: there are no ghostly appearances in this novel, nor any activities quite describable as supernatural. Even so, *Longsword* bids fair to take its place in the gloom-burdened Gothic tradition; and, published in 1762, two years before Horace Walpole's *The Castle of Otranto*, can justly claim to be a forerunner.

In common with Walpole's archetypal fantasy, *Longsword* is set in a period remote from the time when it was written; in *Longsword's* case the England and France of the 1220s, towards the close of the minority of King Henry III. Unlike *The Castle of Otranto*—which depends for its authenticity on the later much-overused device of a wormy old manuscript belatedly dredged to the light and burnished in print—*Longsword* depicts a contemporary narration peopled by a cast of real personalities intermingled with created ones. Much of the novel's merit subsists in its clever combination of the actual and the contrived, the historical and the fictitious, seamlessly blended to create a whole that is both credible and, in many places, shocking. This it does without any recourse to the marvellous: in *Longsword*, we find no talking portraits, as in *Otranto*, no fortuitously tumbling pieces of giant armour. The horror, and there *is* horror, depends upon the cruel connivances of living entities, though the environment in which they operate is often sepulchral enough.

Longsword, Earl of Salisbury represents its author's only known foray into fiction. Thomas Leland was born in Dublin in 1722, and died there in 1785. Educated at the academy of Tom Sheridan (father of dramatist Richard Brinsley Sheridan), young Leland removed to Trinity College Dublin in 1737, and was elected a Fellow in 1746. He was ordained to ministry in the Church of Ireland. In 1754 he co-edited a publication of the *Philippic Orations of Demosthenes*, which included an annotated Latin translation. A version in English came out in 1761. In 1758, Thomas Leland published, in two volumes, his *History of Philip, King of Macedon*. *Longsword, Earl of Salisbury*, which appeared in 1762, seems to have represented something of a touch of light relief, even a quasi-youthful frolic. It is occasionally omitted from Leland's bibliographic listings. In this regard, there is a marked difference from the approach of Horace Walpole, who published the first edition of *Otranto* under a pseudonym, but was happy to assert authorship when the work proved popular. By contrast, Leland never returned to the genre of historical Gothic romance, moving on to commence his *magnum opus*, a *History of Ireland*, which appeared, in three volumes, in 1773. In that year, Leland was appointed vicar of St. Ann's in Dublin, and his ecclesiastical duties seem to have occupied his principal attention for the rest of his life. A three-volume collection of sermons was published posthumously in 1788.

Longsword begins with the landing of the Earl of Salisbury disguised as a cleric on the coast of Cornwall, where he is received by his friend and colleague-in-arms, the elderly knight Randolph. These two had lately fought together in Gascony in a successful bid to embed there the territorial claims of the young English king—Henry III. After departing the coast of France, a storm had dispersed the English fleet, with the ship containing Salisbury presumed lost. However, the warrior earl, together with a small retinue, managed to fetch up on the Isle of Rhè. Salisbury's varied adventures on the island and later on the French mainland, recounted in a long preliminary sub-narrative to Randolph, provide a backdrop for the more sinister misfortunes which lie in store for him closer to home. Subtly repeated references to the old knight's ill-suppressed unease, throughout Salisbury's extended Isle of Rhè story, lead the reader to suspect that this is primarily an appetite-whetter for the worse that lies in wait, although it *does* introduce several personalities vital to the development of the plot. Indeed, much of Leland's skill as an author resides in just this ability to shift perspective and storyline with consummate timing, in tandem unfolding sub-stories and back-narratives, thereby both enhancing suspense and deepening the aura of menace that comes to pervade the entire work. It is a device markedly modern!

Among *Longsword*'s list of actual characters are, not only the much-maligned King John (here presented in somewhat sympathetic mode in a back-history), and his son, the less than resolute King Henry III, but also the pseudonymous Longsword himself. William, styled Longespée, was born in or around 1176, the illegitimate son of King Henry II. (Passing reference is made to this circumstance in the novel.) In 1196, he was married, by his half-brother, then King Richard I, into the distinguished family of Salisbury, taking as his wife, Ela, the third Countess. After the French campaigns of 1225, William Longespée found himself shipwrecked on the Isle of Rhè, where he spent months in hiding in a monastery. (In Leland's novel, Longsword manages only one night in his cloistered retreat before he is lured away, narrowly avoiding a murder attempt.) Longsword's sworn adversary in the novel, Hubert, was another notable of the times. Hubert de Burgh, first Earl of Kent, and younger brother to William de Burgh, Lord of Connaught, was a King John loyalist (even to the point of taking as his second wife the former first spouse of his liege whose marriage had been annulled), and was regent to King Henry III from 1219 until the reaching by that monarch of his majority in 1227. Appointed Justiciar for life in 1228, he fell from favour four years later. Leland takes some historical licence at the end of *Longsword*, when he recounts of his finally victorious hero that his ire "against Lord Hubert was in some degree disarmed, when he received the tidings, that this wicked favourite had forfeited the royal grace, and was ignominiously banished." Despite the novel's muted happy ending (one feels that Ela never quite fully recovered from the ordeal to which she was subjected at the hands of the occupiers of her castle), the real William Longespée died at Salisbury Castle in 1226, not long after his escape from the Isle of Rhè, and while his avowed enemy, Hubert, still stood high in the esteem of the king. For all that the fictional Longsword enjoyed narrow escape from such a fate in the book, rumour ran that Longespée had in truth been poisoned by the contrivance of Hubert de Burgh. In a macabre twist which would have challenged the invention of later Gothic writers, a fact sheet from Salisbury Cathedral has recorded that when the tomb of Longespée was opened in 1791, the preserved body of a rat, discovered to be carrying traces of arsenic, was found in the warlord's skull. The remains of the rat were transferred to a local museum. Maybe there was truth in the old rumours after all, and the wily Hubert enjoyed the last laugh on his redoubtable foe.

Longsword withstands comparison with *Otranto*—and with many a lesser Gothic outpouring—in the stealthy and relentless progressiveness with which the tension is applied. The summarised perils with which *Longsword* opens are martial and brisk, but Leland's novel ratchets into even higher gear when the action transfers to Salisbury Castle and to the point of view of Countess Ela. Here, the bleak genius of Gothic villainy is exemplified in what might be termed a hip-conjoined triumvirate of rogues: the occupying commander, Raymond, nephew to Hubert, an effete, resourceless wretch, spurred as much by lust for Countess Ela as by ambition; his principal courtier, Grey, "a man nurtured in courts; long practised in the arts of flattery, and the homage of dependance; trained to watch the looks, the smiles, the frowns of a superior, to aid his pleasures, to indulge his passions, to love, to hate, as he directed, . . . ever attentive to his own private interest; patient, persevering, and sagacious in the means of advancing it"; and Grey's brother, Reginhald, the Monk. Forerunner to a host of scheming ecclesiastics—not least Matthew Gregory Lewis's flesh-fiend Ambrosio and Ann Radcliffe's conscience-torn confessor, Schedoni— Reginhald, whom we meet only half-way through the book, is presented, by contrast with these others, as a thug in whole cloth, driven by greed, concupiscence, and a wanton fondness for killing. Ever the more eager in villainy, Reginhald is outstripped by his brother only in terms of Grey's sagacious and strategic foreplanning. Much of the novel's strength in terms of plot development derives from the infinite capacity of Grey to duck and dive in various schemes of duplicity according as the rapid shift of events exposes him to the ever recurrent risk of disgrace and death.

While Leland's avoidance of supernatural devices places him in the more sober company of such literary grandees of the dark theme as the sisters Harriet and Sophia Lee and Ann Radcliffe, in the earthiness with which carnal passion is depicted the Dublin-born churchman displays himself no understudy to the excesses of 'Monk' Lewis. At least three condign deaths in *Longsword* come as the result, directly or indirectly, of man's hungering after the body of woman. Of these instances, the following depiction of the carnal appetites of the Monk beggars rival for grossness:

> A country maiden had been seduced to a compliance with his sensual desires. He had for some time consorted with her, 'till by degrees his brutal passion grew sated, and required some new object. He fixed his lascivious eyes upon the concubine of one of his associates in revelling, and made some attempts to possess her; which had provoked her paramour to utter the most violent menaces against the Monk. To appease his resentment, Reginhald basely proposed to give him up the unhappy victim of his own lewdness. The man was not yet so abandoned to all sense of virtue, as not to feel the utmost abhorrence at this instance of transcendent villainy.

For the most part, *Longsword* can be read as an exercise in macabre fiction anchored in the lives of real people from a remote past. Its moral is simply stated: evil prevails at last over good, and when once the hand of weak-willed man is applied to the tiller of wrongdoing, there is no turning back from that course which ultimately will wreck him on the rocks. Only in the sub-narrative of Ela's helpmeet, the widow Elinor (the back-history least pertinent to advancing the story), does one glean, in its recounting of an episode in the strife between King John and the barons, a hint of a concern felt by the author. "O forever accursed be the authors of every civil strife!" ends this sub-story in an outcry, and it is hard to conceive that the appeal glanced lightly from its creator's soul. By the time when *Longsword* was written, the bloody tussle between two contending kings, James II and William III, and their supporters, on Irish soil, had been past for seven decades. Yet perhaps for the compiler of a *History of Ireland*, (dismissed with peevish irreverence in *Anthologia Hibernica* (1794) as "a dull, monotonous detail of domestic convulsions, a weak government, and a barbarous people"), that memory of violent discord among the inhabitants of a shared terrain, had yet the power to linger, and, lingering, still to hurt.

In 1765, *Longsword, Earl of Salisbury* was adapted for the stage by Leland's protégé, and fellow Dubliner, Hall Hartson, under the title *The Countess of Salisbury. A Tragedy.* The play proved to be a notable success. After two years in the Irish capital it transferred to London and was published there in that same year. A new edition came out in 1784, when the title role was played by Sarah Siddons. The play takes considerable licence with the names of characters, and inevitably some are excluded. The action is confined to Salisbury Castle and its environs, with the Isle of Rhè opening story and its aftermath on the French mainland left out altogether. The dramatist, with considerable shrewdness, focuses more on Ela than on her husband. As an adaptation, *The Countess of Salisbury* is effective in reducing the main narrative of *Longsword* to the stage, but much of the novel's more sombre and intricate complexion fails to translate. The character of Grey, still the principal evil advisor to Raymond, relinquishes his versatile villainy in having fewer twists with which to grapple. Reginhald, regrettably, is omitted altogether. Perhaps the peculiar type of the Gothic malefactor succeeds more effectively on the page than the stage. It is instructive, that at the close of Act IV, a planned escape from Salisbury Castle through an underground tunnel (not featured in the novel), demonstrates that at least one of the conventional contrivances of Gothic fiction, manifested in *The Castle of Otranto* in 1764, had been absorbed and applied in Hall Hartson's play a year later.

Thomas Leland's *Longsword*, rich in dark embroidery and deeply imbued with themes of doom and despair, represents both the key to and first portal of the Gothic novel in Ireland. Its freedom from otherworldly revenants allows Leland's sole work of fiction opportunity, that else might have been squandered in redundancy of effect, to explore topics and types which in time would become quintessential to the Gothic. Charles Maturin's tormented *Melmoth the Wanderer*, the vari-shaped spectral soul-persecutors of J. S. Le Fanu, and Bram Stoker's immortal bloodsucking nobleman lay all of them still far in the future—each one strikingly foreshadowed by *Longsword, Earl of Salisbury*, unsung talisman and thaumaturge of the literature of grim gloom.

Albert Power
Killiney, Dublin
June 2012

A Note on the Text

The text of *Longsword* used for this publication is that of the two-volume London edition of 1762, cross-checked on points of accuracy with the single-volume Dublin edition, also of 1762. Archaic spellings have been modernised. The principal editorial interference is in the area of direct speech, where inconsistencies in the use of single and double quotation marks, and the frequent practice of omitting quotation marks either side of the identification of the character speaking, have been rectified to reflect modern usage. Similarly, the mid-eighteenth century practice, in direct speech, of having quotation marks appear at the commencement of every line, has been abandoned in favour of having double quotation marks placed at the start of each paragraph in which character narrative occurs. It is accepted that modern practice would likely substitute an alternative method of differentiating extended passages of direct speech; but it was felt that this would be too excessive an interference with the style favoured by the author and his first publishers. The correlation of closing brackets with other punctuation marks tends to some variance from modern practice, but not so as to cause confusion, and therefore has not been adjusted in the work of editing.

A.P.

*Longsword,
Earl of Salisbury*

Advertisement

The outlines of the following story, and some of the incidents and more minute circumstances, are to be found
in the ancient English historians. If too great liberties
have been taken in altering or enlarging their accounts,
the reader who looks only for amusement will probably
forgive it: the learned and critical (if this work should be
honoured by such readers) will deem it a matter of too
little consequence to call for the severity of their censure.
It is generally expected that pieces of this kind should
convey some one useful moral: which moral, not always
perhaps, the most valuable or refined, is sometimes made
to float on the surface of the narrative; or is plucked up at
proper intervals, and presented to the view of the reader,
with great solemnity. But the author of these sheets hath
too high an opinion of the judgment and penetration of
his readers, to pursue this method. Although he cannot
pretend to be very *deep*, yet he hopes he is *clear*. And if
any thing lies at bottom, worth the picking up, it will be
discovered without his direction.

Book I

SECTION I

When Henry, the third of that name, reigned in England, Sir RANDOLPH, a valiant knight of Cornwall, now too old to take a part in the affairs and commotions of the realm, retired to the peaceful enjoyment of those honours and fortunes, which he had purchased by a series of hardy services in the field. The eve of his life was engaged in the pleasing occupation of training up two youths, his sons, who were rising fast to maturity; in teaching them the sacred duties which they owed to heaven and their country, inspiring them with a gallant love of arms, and possessing their minds with undaunted courage duly tempered with benevolence and humanity.

The season was genial, the evening serene and refreshing; when Randolph wandered forth, with a youth attending him on each side, eagerly listening to his narrative of wars and glorious dangers. The boys passed slowly on, with their eyes and thoughts fixed on their father, 'till they were insensibly led to the brow of a chalky cliff, commanding a wide and uninterrupted view of the calm unruffled sea, that now reflected all the rich and glowing crimson of the setting sun. Here they sat down, and urgently entreated their father to renew the story of his dangers in the Holy Land, the achievements of the brave soldiers of the cross; the recent wars in France, and the valour of Earl Richard and his Knights; while the attention of Randolph was fixed on a small barque, now approaching to the shore.

Its keel cut swiftly and deeply into the sands, and a general shout from the vessel roused the little company, whose attention was still farther awakened, when they observed the deportment of the man who first leaped on shore. His garb was that of an humble pilgrim, whose holy vows were leading him to some scene of devotion; and by his side hung a large and trenchant weapon befitting the son of honourable war, rather than the votary of religion; his look was pale and squalid; but his port erect; and a secret greatness and manly dignity seemed to break through all the gloom of adversity which surrounded him. No sooner had he touched the strand, than he stood for a moment, as it were, in a still and motionless surprise; then falling on his knees, with arms crossed, and eyes raised up to heaven, his looks expressed the most rapturous gratitude and thankfulness, as if for a deliverance from some great calamity; whilst some others of the crew, with all appearances of tender regard, conveyed a young and beautiful personage to shore, dressed in the same habit with their leader. The whole scene was extraordinary and affecting: the youths had descried it, and starting up, and turning to their father, seemed to demand the reason of this appearance. "Come, my sons," cried Randolph, "this stranger appears unfortunate; perhaps he may accept of our hospitable reception; let our friendly offices not be wanting, to allay his grief, and to supply his necessities." Thus saying, he led them by a winding descent towards the shore, where the crew were by this time disembarked.

Sir Randolph approached the stranger, (to whom the rest of the company seemed to pay a particular regard) with a concern truly humane: when, instantly, the eyes of each were fixed in mute surprise upon the other.—"My

General!"—"My Knight!" Their tongues could utter no more: they rushed into each other's arms, and clung together in a tumultuous disorder of grief, amazement, and affection. At length, words forced their passage. "Great Earl!" cried Randolph, "and do I really behold thee? Do I embrace the man, under whose command my last days of honourable war saw glory and victory? Hath my leader survived the dreadful night of tempest which dispersed our ships! He whom we imagined buried in the seas! Is he at length returned in safety? But why this garb? Are these wretched weeds, befitting the son of an illustrious monarch, the conqueror of Gascoigne, the glory of England? Thou art come, but not to peace and repose: danger, difficulty, and distress, are still prepared for that undaunted spirit!"—"Am I not in England?" replied the stranger. "Have I not, at length, happily escaped the insidious attempts of my enemies? What dangers have I now to fear? No, my dearest ELA! illustrious dame! tenderest wife! In thy arms shall I now forget my dangers. To thee I fly, to wipe away those tears, which burst forth at my departure, and must have flowed in full streams, during this melancholy interval of my absence. In thee and thy endearments shall all my future hopes be centred: and never, no, nevermore shall WILLIAM be deluded by the smiling promises of glory, to hazard the chance of arms! Enough hath been already done: enough hath been given to honour and to my country. Peace and retirement, repose and tranquillity be now the lot of these shattered limbs, and this distracted, wearied, spirit!"

Whilst the Earl thus indulged his flattering prospects of tranquillity, the thoughts of Randolph were busy and disordered; he surveyed him with a mixture of pity and affection; and half suppressing the sigh that laboured in his breast, he assumed a look of ease and complacency, and invited Lord William and his attendants to partake of the refreshment which his neighbouring residence afforded. They passed on with the pleasing sensations of men, who after a length of days spent in a foreign and unfriendly land, began once more to taste the comforts of a native country, and to share in the social intercourse of kinsmen and fellow citizens. Their leader turned to the youthful pilgrim, whom he embraced with a tender and affectionate concern; but with such joy as seemed clouded by the remembrance of past calamities. They retired a few paces as if in private conference, and the elder seemed intent in comforting and encouraging. The courteous Knight would not break in upon their private conference, and to leave them the more free to indulge that mutual affection which they discovered, he turned to his youths: "Behold," said he, "this truly honourable Lord, great in descent, powerful in arms; full of the mighty spirit of his royal father the second Henry, a monarch fatally seduced by the beauty of Rosamund: and (mark the just dispensations of heaven) heavy was the punishment which the mother paid, for her forbidden love: nor hath misfortune spared this the offspring of an unlawful and unhappy passion. Yet let us be just to his virtues; and learn from him, that renown is not to be purchased but by toil and perils. Under his banners hath your father oftentimes encountered dangers. With him did I hasten to support the cause and title of our King, when John had met his fate, and the son of France rioted in the calamities of England. With him did these old arms contribute to execute the vengeance of our country upon the adherents of the perfidious Lewis; and when the Count Mal-leon revolted from his liege lord, and erected the standard of France in our province of Gascoigne, then did he bravely second the efforts of Richard, uncle to our Prince, and led us on to victory. Aspire to the same renown: but expect the like fortune: dream not of undisturbed happiness and tranquillity. By expecting labour and distress, you shall learn to encounter, and to conquer them, in a glorious and honest cause."

Thus far paternal tenderness diverted the attention of Randolph from his illustrious friend, who in this short interval had been equally engaged. He embraced his followers, congratulated their happy arrival, and zealously extolled their merits and faithful services. The Knight, with all due courtesy, led them on towards his hospitable hall, which soon opened to their view, and soon received the wearied guests. No friendly care was wanting to recall their languid and drooping spirits. As men just snatched from the dread gulph of misery, and suddenly restored to a degree of happiness beyond the hopes and even the conceptions of their dejected thoughts, they gazed each upon his fellow in a silent ecstasy of surprise and joy; and still more endeared to each other, as sharers in the same misfortunes, their eyes, their hands encountered spontaneously, and they embraced with an affecting cordiality and pleasure. Earl William, who now began to resume his native dignity, his eyes, as it were, newly lighted up, his voice less plaintive, his aspect greater, and his port still more princely, earnestly seized the hand of that young personage, to whom he seemed more particularly attentive, and thus addressed himself to his host. "O, my friend, here is our dearest charge. Know, and respect this beautiful maid, for such she is, the daughter of a brave and honest soldier. His name Les Roches, and once mine enemy: but fortune and his virtues united us in bands of friendship, truly sacred and inviolable. It is his goodness that I now see my native land. His generous pity saved me when the arm of mine enemy was just raised to strike, to strike me basely, and treacherously, unknowing, unsuspecting, and unprovided for defence." "Welcome, Lady," replied the Knight; "alas! these limbs were not formed for toil or dangerous adventure. But where is thy gallant father? My heart pants to embrace him; an English heart, which holds a soldier dear, of whatever clime or country: and doubly dear, and doubly honoured, shall that soldier be, who restores a noble and beloved son to England." Here grief threatened to break through the fair reserve of female modesty; and had already fallen in gentle drops, down her glowing cheeks; which the Earl perceiving, checked with a kindly reproving look; then softly entreated Randolph to summon such of his domestics as might be proper to conduct her to refreshment and repose. These instantly appeared, and were instructed to perform their offices with all tender and respectful care. The maid retired in silence: Randolph seemed wrapt in delight and wonder, whilst the Earl pursued her parting steps with looks of sweetest complacency and pity. The Knight then turning to the followers of this Lord, "My friends," said he, "your toils demand retirement: this roof knows no other happiness than to greet the approach of worth and valour. It is yours, and use it freely. For this night, at least, forget your labours, and indulge your faint and harassed limbs in peaceful rest."—"Yes," said the Earl, "to rest, my dear companions; but, bear with my impatience, and be stirring with the dawn; that we may issue forth with new-recruited speed, and quickly gain my castle. There shall our labours end; there shall the gentle Countess acknowledge your deserts; and there shall her long lost Lord reward your fidelity.—Sir Randolph, you too shall accompany us, and share the general joy. We shall teach you to receive your fellow-soldier with a more lively sympathy, and brighten that honest aspect with gayer smiles."

To this gentle reproof, which seemed to have escaped unwarily from the jealousy of friendship, Randolph made no reply; but with a countenance of strict composure, which effectually concealed whatever thoughts or passions were now busy in his mind, he invited Lord William to retire. "No, my friend," replied the Earl,—"my followers are happily disposed of: at last (thanks to the preserving hand of Heaven, and to thee) they enjoy that secure repose, to which they have been so long strangers. I feel my heart eased of its oppressing load. Nor will I give these to sleep, till I have heard—Say, what of my wife, what of my friends, of the King and realm, can my good host impart?—But chiefly of my wife; of Ela I would hear all thou canst deliver; how hath she borne this tedious absence? Knowest thou not of her present state? Speak! alas, the grief of my widowed dame seems to affect that good heart. But say, is she well"—Randolph had betrayed some agitation at these enquiries; but quickly recollecting his disordered thoughts, "her tenderness and love for thee hath been approved," said he, "in the absence of her Lord: tomorrow thou shalt seek her in her princely castle. But now indulge my impatience: say, what means this garb? this appearance of misfortune? Who are these thy attendants?"—"Yes," said the Earl, "I will tell thee all. Sit down.—Thou wilt not be displeased to hear the story of my misfortunes since our last dreadful separation." Randolph obeyed, and the Earl thus began.

SECTION II

"How can I recall to mind the fatal time, when our victorious army, loaded with the spoils of Gascoigne, re-embarked, and with hearts of joy and expectation, steered towards their native shore. Thou, Randolph, who hadst shared the dangers of our war, whose hoary head still disdained to droop beneath its beaver, must retain the dreadful remembrance of that night, when winds and seas conspired together, and united their unrelenting fury against the bands of England: when the roaring hurricane deafened us with its horrid menaces, and the frequent lightning served to disclose all the terrors of the gloomy deep. Our army, that had undauntedly defied the swords of France, found now another enemy, against whose obstinate assaults their courage seemed but ineffectual: and every moment presented us with the distracting expectation of perishing in dishonourable obscurity. And much doth it rejoice me, that in that extremity of distress, the blessed saints were not unmindful of Randolph, that my gallant knight was happily rescued from destruction, to cheer his friends, and enjoy his latter days in peace and dignity. The fate of Salisbury was more severe and affecting. The ship which received me and my associates was quickly separated from our fleet, a helpless and solitary prey to the violence of the tempest, which our pilot had neither skill nor spirit to oppose. And in that dreadful moment, when, raised to a giddy and terrible height, we hung upon the breaking wave, or sunk down deep into the dark and yawning gulph, then was my heart's dear treasure, my beloved dame, present to my distracted mind: to die was horrible; because to die was to be torn from Ela. Her sorrows crowded upon my busy fancy; and I sunk; O, my friend, how can I speak it! I sunk into a coward.—Doth that tear now stealing down your furrowed cheek express your pity of my weakness, or a sense of my misfortunes?"—The disorder of the good Knight, which could no longer be entirely concealed, here suspended the narration. Lord William seized his hand with a look of surprise and concern at his sensibility: but Randolph prevented all expostulation, by a sudden and violent effort to resume his serenity. He soon recalled his thoughts to a composed attention, and at his desire the Earl proceeded.

"Heaven was at length pleased in some degree to control the violence of the storm. The dawn of morning seemed to promise us at least some respite from destruction: yet still, helpless and desponding, without course or direction, we tossed as the winds and tides impelled: and when at last we descried land, that cheering object to wretches who have supported an unequal contest with the raging tempest, only served to inspire us with new fears, lest it should prove the land of our enemy. But alas! it was decreed (and the shocking scene still dwells on my imagination in all its horror) that far the greater part of us should never touch the shore which lay in view. We steered upon a coast utterly unknown: the rock which lay in ambush to destroy us, assailed our vessel; the waves rushed impetuously through the breach. In that dreadful moment, when hope vanished, when Death stood with open arms to receive his prey, the magnanimity of my dear unhappy companions—how shall I speak it! They clung round my knees with tears of solicitude and zeal for my preservation. They entreated, they pressed, they forced me to seek for safety in the boat, which it was their last care to make ready for their beloved captain, with ten more the most eminent in command. Resolute and undismayed even in the very moment of their destruction, they hailed our departure and triumphed in our safety. I hear their shouts! they still strike my ears.—O England! can the world boast such sons?—The deep closed over them, and snatched the dear, afflicting, aweful object forever from our eyes. We rowed away in silence and astonishment, full of the terrible idea, and little cheered by the prospect of land, which we dreaded to find unfriendly. Nor were our fears mistaken: for when our last and utmost efforts had been exerted to gain the shore, some wretched fishermen who had at first gazed in expectation on our vessel, and at the sight of armed men, fled precipitately into the country, appeared by their garb and language to be French, and convinced us that the prospect of immediate destruction, was only changed for another no less dreadful, that of an hard and tedious captivity: that of falling into the hands of men whom we had but now defied and vanquished; and being made the victims of revenge for blood still reeking upon our blades.

"We moored our boat, uncertain what course to pursue, whether to seek refuge from our enemies in an unknown and tempestuous sea, or by advancing forward to resign ourselves into their power. It was, however, soon resolved boldly to meet our danger. We moved on slowly and circumspect; the sun played upon our armour, and its reflected beams served as a direction to a small armed band that had been alarmed by their countrymen, and now marched forth to seek their invaders. My companions, little dismayed at such a superiority of numbers as they had frequently repelled, unsheathed their swords, now their only weapons, and stood, as men resolved to defend their lives and liberty to the utmost. The undaunted show of resistance persuaded our enemies that some hostile design was meditated, and that greater numbers were approaching to our support. They halted and surveyed us: their bowmen discharged their shafts; and three of my unhappy friends lay bleeding upon the earth, pouring out their lives without a possibility of assistance, or the consolation of a brave revenge. Our enemies, animated by their success, rushed upon us; they felt our blades; but soon taught us that resistance was ineffectual. They surrounded my friends, and impatient to secure their captives, hurried them precipitately across the plain; but in their blind unguided fury, left me at some distance singly engaged with their commander, who with couched lance, spurred forward, and loudly called upon me to yield my-self his prisoner, or meet my fate. Active and experienced in arms, I evaded his onset, and with this good sword (whose length and keenness had long been the terror of his countrymen) I aimed a blow, which was received by his fiery charger. The beast grew furious with anguish, and impatient of command soon cast his rider at my feet. But I, who neither inclined, nor deemed it prudent to pursue the work of death; ever ready to spare a prostrate foe, and nothing disposed to provoke a severe vengeance on my companions; lifted my beaver, and with looks of courtesy raised the leader from the ground. I prepared to accost him, when, starting back, as if unable to support some sudden and violent surprise; he stood speechless and mo-tionless, casting his eyes to heaven, and fixing them on me by turns. 'Blessed Saints!—O noble Lord!'—thus did he exclaim; 'Twice my preserver! How shall Les Roches repay thy exalted goodness? In the Isle of Rhè! and thus attend-ed! But fly this moment; I must rejoin my friends. That path is safe: it leads thee to a place of concealment: expect me soon; and expect some return of gratitude.'

"With these words, the stranger (for such he still seemed to me) turned hastily away, in pursuit of his troop, now leading off their prisoners in triumph. Nor could I suddenly recover from my amazement. Mine eyes still attended him, and marked his hasty steps, until he was lost in the distant crowd. Then suddenly recollecting mine own danger, and his friendly counsel, I took the path to which he had pointed, and measured out the tedious way with limbs wearied and faint, and with a mind no less harassed by tumultuous passions. Still confounded and perplexed, my thoughts sought in vain for that security, that concealment which the stranger had promised; when turning mine eyes eagerly on every side in search of some cheering object, they at length discovered at some distance a large and venerable pile. Its windows crowded with the foliage of their ornaments, and dimmed by the hand of the painter; its numerous spires towering above the roof, and the Christian ensign on its front, declared it a residence of devotion and charity. Hither I determined to bend my course, and to fix here, my last and only hopes of refuge. War had long taught me to support toil and abstinence. But, alas! my spirit now denied its wonted assistance to my exhausted strength, and when my limbs had laboured up the eminence on which this mansion stood, with slow and painful efforts; when a few paces only remained to bring me to the entrance, nature could struggle no farther; my sight grew clouded, I fell, as in the arms of death, and fainted under the severe oppression of fatigue and distress. Nor did my miserable state escape the regards of charity; for when my languid eyes again opened to the light, I found myself attended by one who seemed an inhabitant; and from him learnt that I lay before the portal of an ancient Abbey, where the brethren of the Cistertian order, employed their peaceful hours in orisons to heaven, and acts of humanity to their fellow creatures. The friendly door was laid open for my reception: the arm which had raised me from the ground, with the same humane concern supported my tottering steps, and led me through the winding aisles, to a retired chamber; where the charitable offices of my attendant were busily employed to provide whatever might be needful for rest and refreshment, whatever might recall the strength or comfort the afflicted spirit of a wretched stranger.

"I felt the kind effects of his pious care; and though still anxious and oppressed, yet relieved from the extremity of languor, and conscious of returning strength, I requested to be conducted to the Reverend Abbot; who in that instant prevented me, and entered, to enquire into the occasion of my arrival, and to know what further offices might be granted to a man, whose appearance and distress had by this time engaged the attention of the whole fraternity. With the authority of a superior, he directed my conductor to withdraw, and for a while surveyed me with a kind yet piercing eye. His aspect, from which the beams of piety and charity seemed to break forth in a mild and cheering light, commanded reverence and love. I made the due obeisance, and entreated his kind protection for a man who had drank deeply of affliction, who stood before him a monument of the tremendous displeasure of heaven, torn, perhaps forever, from all that he held dear, cast on a foreign shore, without guide, friend, or refuge: yet, sometime, no stranger to happier days. 'Son!' replied the venerable father, 'these gates are never barred against the afflicted: but far be all pollution from our walls! War hath been thy occupation: but hath that sword ever been stained with the blood of a friend or brother? Hath no great offence odious to religion or humanity, cut thee off from society; and driven thee away a wretched and abandoned wanderer?' Impatient of suspicion, I fell upon my knees before him, and instantly addressed myself to shrift; opened my whole soul freely, as in the face of heaven, declared my country, my name and quality; and distinctly recounted my late unhappy fortunes. The good father heard me with exact attention; hesitating and struggling with the rising passion, he uttered some words of comfort, while the big tear rolled down: nor did this mark of generous pity disgrace his venerable aspect; although he laboured to conceal it, when he was to urge the precepts of fortitude and patience. 'My son!' said he (now resuming a look of ease and composed dignity), 'Nature obliges us to feel, but Religion forbids us to repine. That Power which deals out misfortune to sinful mortals, will, in his own appointed time, accept of their penitence, and wipe away their tears. Thou art the enemy of my country, but thou art a man. This roof shall not yet reject thee: retire and rest securely: the duties of my office call me: with tomorrow's rising sun I will revisit thee.' He departed; and deprived me of that momentary comfort, which his looks and voice inspired.

"The couch now received me, but not to repose. My busy thoughts, too long and too violently agitated to subside into serenity and quiet, revolved the dreadful scenes in which I had been just now engaged: sometimes were they fixed on the fate of my companions; now, on my own danger: and ever and anon distracted me with the recollection of my country, my family, and (O killing torment!) my wife. But I was not long permitted to indulge these sad reflections. A rude knocking at the gates echoed through the arched aisles, and roused me from my gloomy dreams. Suddenly it ceased. Silence, still more alarming, and anxious expectation succeeded. I started up, and grasped my sword as it were instinctively. I heard the feet of haste approaching my chamber. The door opened, and there stood before me the Frenchman, whose life I had that day spared: and whom I now recognised rather by his voice, than by the glimmering lamp depending from the ceiling. 'Have I found my preserver?' (thus did he earnestly accost me) 'well did I divine that he would find refuge with my reverend kinsman: and that I should still be able to repay the goodness of Lord William'—'Thou knowest me,' said I, hastily interrupting him; 'twice, I think, thou saidst, twice I had preserved thee. All this is strange, and would be unfolded.' 'Recall to mind,' replied the Frenchman, 'that busy day, when the gallant Earl of Marche was forced to yield before the English bands led by Duke Richard and by thee. The impetuous Mal-leon, he, whose envy of thy superior worth and greatness had first prompted him to revolt from England, he who hated thy name, and sickened at the report of thy valour, loudly defied and challenged thee: ye engaged, horse to horse, with the furious rage of rivals; and soon the superior prowess of Salisbury prevailed.' 'I well remember it,' said I; 'and when the Count was sinking to the ground, a valiant soldier rushed forward to his rescue; and exposed himself to all the fury of his victorious enemies.' 'I was that soldier,' cried he: 'mine own men shrunk cowardly from me, the English surrounded me, and when their swords were raised to destroy me; then did Lord William with difficultly repress their violence, and I became his prisoner.'—Here I interrupted him—'A prisoner! then were my intentions not duly executed. That fidelity and valour which prompted the brave soldier to defy the terrors of death in order to preserve his friend, deserved more respect and better fortune. My orders were that he should be freed and honourably conducted to his own camp without delay or ransom.' 'And these orders were obeyed,' said he; 'I was freed, I was honourably conducted to my own camp without delay or ransom: and there did I loudly proclaim thy worth. The listening soldiers hung on me with rapture whilst I told the deed: and enemies were taught to revere the magnanimity and generous humanity of England and of Salisbury. O fatal zeal of gratitude! The Count Mal-leon whose imperious spirit could but ill endure the piercing wound his honour had now received; discomfited, disgraced, and doubly conquered, now felt the most malignant passions rankling in his breast: tortured by the praises of the conqueror, he breathed revenge and fury; thundered out the severest and most tremendous menaces against himself, the world, but above all against Lord

William. O! would to heaven that this extravagance of rage and malice had even now subsided!' Here the good Frenchman seemed in no small emotion, raised, as I then conceived, by the ardour of gratitude and indignation at the ungenerous conduct of his countryman. I endeavoured to divert him to some other subject, by discovering an unwillingness of hearing my own commendations, and by speaking of the malice of my enemy with slight and scorn. 'Alas,' said he, 'thou knowest not half thy danger. In this island on which thou hast been cast naked and defenceless, Count Savourè de Mal-leon bears an absolute command. If he should discover thee (which heaven forbid!) what fortunate event could save thy life? or if spared, what ransom could purchase thy liberty? I am indeed his officer, but all my cares and services must be devoted to my preserver. Thy remaining friends I have seen disposed, with such advantage as their present state allows. Their ransom shall be my work; but O, my heart bleeds for their noble leader! I chose this silent hour, when darkness might conceal me from the eye of suspicion, to come and warn thee of thy danger. Let these holy walls still conceal thee: nor dare to brave the arm of revenge and malice. I must retire: thy friends shall be my care: and may heaven direct me to some means of speedily removing thee from this accursed place!' I seized the hand of the generous Les Roches, and attempted to express my acknowledgement of his humane and noble friendship: but he hastily broke from me with a tender and affecting prayer for my preservation; and left me full of wonder and perplexity."

SECTION III

"The lingering hours of night at length passed away, and the Mattin-bell summoned the reverend fraternity to their early devotions. Their pious cares for me were now renewed, their charitable offices repeated, to oblige and comfort me. The hoary Abbot returned to cheer me with his presence, and his ghostly counsel. I was witness of the comforts of religion and tranquillity. Happiness seemed to me the native resident of the cloister; and my repining heart murmured against heaven that had marked me out for the storm and turbulence of life. Another day was spent, and another night passed away more tranquil and refreshing: and I rose with my thoughts fixed on the kind Les Roches, and in anxious impatience for his return. The day advanced, but my friend still delayed his coming. At length the charitable Abbot appeared, not with a front of placid serenity, but gloomy and contracted, full of anxiety and grief, which like the infectious blast that at once destroys the fruits of nature, filled my soul instantly with I knew not what dreadful and ominous presage. 'Unhappy son!' said he; 'Mal-leon has discovered, if not the place of thy concealment, at least that thou art concealed in this island: thanks to the indiscretion of some of thy countrymen which disclosed the name of their commander. His jealousy points to Les Roches as the author of thy escape: vengeance is denounced against him; and this moment the good Les Roches lies in the damp dungeon.' 'For me!' said I: 'And is charity so great a crime? Is tyranny suffered to rage thus without control in France? For me doth my kind preserver endure the pains of captivity?'—With a look in which affection and authority were united, the father here repressed my emotion. 'Son,' said he, 'the time calls for calm and determined measures. In this place thou can'st not longer abide. Thy coming was not secret, and should it reach Mal-leon, alas, I fear the impetuosity of that proud Count might drive him to violate the sacred privileges of our house. Les Roches, though now unable to assist thee, is yet anxious still for thy preservation. The peasant sent by him to inform me of thy dangers waits to conduct thee faithfully to the vessel prepared to convey thee to Rochelle. Thither thy ransomed friends have already directed their course; and from thence some fortunate event may conduct thee to thy native country. Tarry here, until the shades of night may conceal thy departure. Then issue forth: and may all good angels hold thee in their protection! Our prayers'—Here pity stopped his voice; and filled his eyes with tears; whilst I in broken accents laboured to express my sense of his goodness, my pity for the kind and injured Les Roches, and my indignation at the baseness of Mal-leon. He saw my passionate disorder; he entreated, he exhorted, and he reproved; till perceiving by my wandering and inattention, that my mind was too busily engaged to admit his spiritual counsels, he retired and abandoned me to my own reflections; and these were entirely confined to the misfortunes of the generous and kind Les Roches. I accused myself as the sole author of his sufferings; and abhorred the mean design of flying, when I had involved my friend in danger. What can the malice of Mal-leon inflict on me (it was thus I reasoned) if to purchase the liberty of my preserver, I resign myself into his power? To kill me!—That were unnatural. The man I never injured cannot proceed to such an extravagance of calm unprovoked cruelty. Or if he could, my country could not long be unacquainted with my fate; and would (he must be well assured) discharge all its vengeance on my destroyer. And shall the fear of bearing the insult and triumph of my rival in arms, shall the tediousness of captivity or the severities of a prison, drive me from the man who suffers for his goodness towards me? Shall I sacrifice his freedom, perhaps his life, only to hasten my return to England?—The thought appeared odious and dishonourable. I instantly formed the daring resolution of purchasing the freedom of Les Roches, by delivering myself into the hands of my enemy; and spent the remaining hours of day in that satisfaction and complacency which arise from the flattering ideas of self-applause. The sun declined; darkness gradually prevailed, and at length brought on the hour of my departure. And now, firmly and obstinately settled in my dangerous purpose, I received the benediction of the reverend Abbot, with a countenance of fixed serenity, which he, good man, commended, as an indication of my reliance upon heaven. Touched with his goodness, I could not suppress the tears that started from me and interrupted my grateful acknowledgements of his charitable care, and his zealous prayers for my protection. Our hands were clasped in each other; our eyes rather than our tongues spoke the emotions of our breasts, until the father, who first made the effort to repress his passion, urged the necessity of my departure: and while he ardently commended me to every holy saint, I issued forth under the direction of the peasant my conductor.

"I had not departed many paces from the Abbey, when addressing myself to the guide, with a voice which bespoke a deliberate and determined resolution, I commanded him to conduct me to the prison where Les Roches lay confined. The poor man, who was no stranger to my quality or to my hazardous situation, expressed the utmost horror and astonishment; and in language rude and unrefined, yet such as denoted an honest and a tender affection, attempted to remonstrate against such a perilous design. I showed him gold; but this had no effect. I then drew my sword, and threatened him with the utmost severity of vengeance, unless he instantly obeyed my command. Terror seemed to have a greater influence than entreaties or promises. He changed his course and called on me to follow. Thus directed, I eagerly took the path which I supposed would lead me to my friend; filled with the high thoughts of obtaining his freedom by a free resignation of my own. But after long traversing the gloomy and tedious way, I found too late that either fear and darkness had misled my conductor, or that he had purposely deceived my expectations; for when the dawn began to appear, we found ourselves suddenly prevented from all farther progress by a deep and rapid current. The peasant trembled: but I had no power (however irritated) to punish his error, or his mistaken tenderness. Exhausted as I was, with fatigue and inward agitation, my arm with difficulty took the casque from my forehead. I dipped it in the stream, and drank deeply; then resigning my feeble limbs to the dank ground, insensible of all danger, and indifferent to my fate, I sunk into a profound sleep, nor did I awaken till the meridian sun flashed upon me with its beams and roused me by the full force of their heat and brightness. I called on the peasant; but he had deserted me. I arose, and wandered slowly along the banks of the river, without purpose or direction: and so freely did I indulge the wandering of my thoughts, so far was I lost to recollection, that I never once perceived the sound of approaching feet, till I was encompassed by six armed men, who proved, as I at once supposed, the guards of Count Mal-leon.—But, my friend, why should I abuse thy indulgence, by this minute detail? Night steals fast from us. Let me not forget what thy age demands." "No," replied Randolph, "think not of me; my soul is all attention to the misfortunes of my leader. Haste and give to my impatience the story of thy deliverance, that I too, in my turn, may relate the things which demand thy serious ear."—The Earl then proceeded.

SECTION IV

"The soldiers required my name, my purpose, and destination: and as I had long since resigned all hopes of escape, I discovered myself without reserve or difficulty. Two of them were instantly dismissed with a nod, and departed with the most precipitate speed; whilst the remaining number, with that courtesy and respect, which bespoke them the brave and generous sons of honourable war, conducted me to a cottage that lay at some small distance, fast by the margin of the current. Here was I treated, not with imperious insolence, the effect of base and dishonourable enmity, but with all humane and kind regards due to a brave unfortunate. This encouraged me to attempt some conference with my keepers; who, on their part, discovered no reluctance to gratify their prisoner. From them I learned that my guide had really mistaken the way, and that I now lay within one hour's distance from the castle of their Lord. I earnestly enquired after the fate of Les Roches, and heard with a mixture of joy, and vexation at my own precipitate conduct, that on the preceding night, he had been released from his captivity. When I expressed my surprise and satisfaction at this event, I was told that immediately after the surviving Englishmen had been ransomed by the bounty of Les Roches, and suffered, at his intercession, to depart, Count Savourè had received information that one of them had rashly discovered, that the Lord of Salisbury, their leader, was still in the Isle of Rhè! This instantly kindled up a flame of passion in his breast. He affected to regard the tale of their distress as vain and fictitious; and expressed strong apprehensions of a conspiracy formed by his enemies in concert with his officer to seize the island. In this sudden and violent fit of rage, he had commanded Les Roches to prison, and ordered a strict guard to watch round the coast. The Frenchman, conscious of his own innocence, exclaimed loudly against the severity of his commander; mentioned the inconsiderable number of the Englishmen that had appeared, and enlarged on the unreasonable nature of the Count's suspicions. He demanded to know, if any man had dared to accuse him; if he had an accuser, he defied him to the lists, and offered to prove his falsehood and his own loyalty in single combat. Yet with what reserve so ever these soldiers spoke of their commander, I learned clearly that his remonstrances had not so great an effect on Count Savourè, as the power and insolence of Les Roches, who though he fought under his command, had himself a numerous and formidable body of feudatory vassals, that attended him in arms, and were attached to their chief with an ardent and invariable affection. It appeared plainly, that fear (for cruel natures are most accessible to fear) had determined the imperious Count to release my friend, when the first sudden passion of rage had somewhat abated, and no appearance of danger had been discovered. My guards informed me still farther, that on this very morning, Mal-leon had repented of his lenity; and that his apprehensions were again awakened, as he had received information that on that part of the shore which looks towards the mainland of France, another vessel had been discovered hovering about the island, with an appearance which fully warranted suspicion. I readily concluded that this was no other than the vessel in which my ransomed friends had embarked, and which still lay off the shore in hopes of receiving me. But without discovering this, I contented myself with earnestly disavowing, in general, all intentions of an hostile nature; nor could I speak of the mean fears and insolent severity of Mal-leon but with a warm and passionate indignation. But here our conference was interrupted by the arrival of another body, who came, as they said, to take charge of me, and dismissed the others from their attendance. I now expected to be led in triumph to the presence of my enemy, but soon learned that I was to continue for some time in my present situation. At this I ventured to express some surprise. But the looks and words of sullen gloom and moroseness which these my new guards assumed, obliged me to suppress all farther enquiries. I submitted patiently to my fate. I was disarmed, and confined in the cottage under the care of two soldiers who seemed to command the party, the rest of which they had disposed at some distance, in different situations, to watch all approaches that might threaten rescue.

"Night advanced upon us, and I was left to my repose: but what repose remained for a wretch tossed about through all the vicissitudes of danger, toil, and distress, by the capricious cruelty of fortune? A thousand thoughts and a thousand passions encountered each other in my distracted breast. I threw myself upon my hard and homely couch; and started up by turns; like the feverish wretch, incessantly changing, in fruitless search of ease. Nature seemed to lour upon me, and to thunder terror into my affrighted ears: the loud storm and the roaring torrent broke in upon the silence of night, and made darkness doubly dreadful. How did I then accuse the slow and indolent advances of time, that tortured me with cruel delay? Oftentimes did I endeavour to compose my troubled thoughts; and as often did the terrors of the night awaken my distractions. Watchful and disordered as I was, my soul was soon tortured with a new and terrible alarm. It was now the dead midnight hour: on that side where my chamber looked down upon the troubled river, I plainly heard my two guards in dreadful conference, encouraging each other to the horrid purpose of murder. 'It is now,' said one, 'the very moment of execution; he sleeps: take you this dagger, and let us enter: when we have dispatched this Englishman, my orders are to plunge his body in the river, that it may be thought he has escaped: observe me well: and be assured of the favour of our Count. The dagger is the last resource. No blood if possible: our first attempt must be by strangling.' "—"Accursed wretch!" cried Randolph, with a sudden and violent interruption: "what was the crime of Salisbury? Is superior worth so odious and insupportable? Can envy prove so bloody?"—"Oftentimes," said Lord William, "have I seen death loading the fields of war with frightful carnage: and never did my soul shrink at his approach: but now when he appeared in the form of a calm and deliberate assassin, I at once lost all firmness. The cold dew issued from every pore; I commended myself to heaven; and lay entranced in dismay. A hideous interval of suspense succeeded, for the murderers had not yet appeared. The torture of this delay was even worse than death. To this I had resigned myself, or even wished to receive it. Still I lay in stupid expectation of the fatal messengers of death; and still their horrid deed was suspended. A sudden and violent tumult recalled my dying senses, the noise grew nearer and louder. I started at the clash of arms: I heard a groan. The crowd pressed in upon me, and I saw Les Roches, my kind preserver, his eyes darting rage, and his weapon reeking with slaughter. 'There lies the wretch,' said he, 'who dared to lift his sword against my approach.' I threw myself into his bloody arms; in a rapturous ecstasy of joy and gratitude, and just found breath to exclaim, 'Gracious powers! am I then rescued from the base murderer's arm?' 'Murder!' cried Les Roches; 'for this horrid purpose then wer't thou detained here! But it is well: there wanted but this to confirm those brave spirits, who feel and will revenge our wrongs. No prisoner now! No concealed fugitive! Lord William shall confront his enemy; and take his free course, undaunted and uncontrolled in the fair face of day; and scorn the malice of this injurious Count. But haste—and let us join our friends.'

"I obeyed the joyful summons; but first searched for my armour, which the guards, whose power was now expired, had taken from me. The attendants of Les Roches buckled on my harness, and I once more grasped my sword. I issued forth as if restored from the grave, accompanied by Les Roches and his companions, leading away my guards whom they had overpowered. And scarcely had we measured out the distance of an arrow's flight, when we descried a gallant troop marching towards us, who raised a shout of triumph at our approach, and received us with the joy of brethren and associates. I expressed my surprise, but was soon taught the reason of this appearance, and the cause of my surprising change of fortune. I now learned that Mal-leon, like the unskilful soldier who by the force of his own ill-directed blow is oftentimes tumbled to the ground, was defeated in the purposes of his malice, by the blind and furious impetuosity of that very malice. In his first rage of disappointed revenge, he had injured and insulted a brave chief; who had ranged his numerous adherents under the banners of this proud Count, and given their swords to support his power. The gentle manners of Les Roches had ever commanded the affections of his adherents, and now, when they saw their chief thrust into the vile dungeon, in contempt of all his former services; and for no crime, but the suspicion of having spared an helpless wanderer, their mutiny, like the noise of distant thunder, though not violent, was yet terrible; and struck the ear with the threatenings of an approaching storm. Mal-leon quickly perceived the danger, and endeavoured to correct his hasty error, by releasing Les Roches from his captivity. But little did this ungracious condescension allay the ferment of his vassals, little did their chief regard this extorted act of justice, as the reparation due to his injured honour, and little did it allay the ardour of his affection and solicitude for the man he now called his friend. It was his first care to employ the liberty he had regained, in my protection; and with a few chosen followers he instantly hastened to the shore whither he had directed the faithful peasant to conduct me. But Salisbury was not to be found. Yet still flattered with the hopes that my speed had prevented him, and that I had already embarked, he returned with his attendants, to whom he distinctly related our first encounter in the island, and his cares to defend me from the malice of my rival. They were taught to love me, to pity my fortunes, and to rejoice in my supposed escape. The infection spread among their associates. I became the general object of their discourse; when suddenly, the peasant who had fled from me in wild affright, to inform his master of my situation, arrived and acquainted them, that, amidst all my dangers, I had obstinately resolved not to abandon my friend, but to share his fortune; in despite of all the power and cruelty of Mal-leon. Scarcely had he informed them of his own error, and the place where he had left me, when the news arrived of my being seized, and detained until the Count might declare his pleasure. Not the flashing lightning when it has broken in upon a forest of our stately oaks, ever raised a more sudden and violent conflagration, than these accounts kindled in the minds of the brave soldiers of Les Roches. It was at once resolved forever to abandon the service of a tyrannical and revengeful Lord, and to rescue me from his oppressive power. But their chief wisely laboured to temper and allay the violence which threatened to defeat its own purpose.

By his persuasion it was determined to act with secrecy and caution: to wait until darkness might conceal their motions, and to choose the dead hour of midnight, to surprise my guards, and to snatch me from the cruel malice of my enemy. Eternal goodness! that directed their hearts, and guided their steps, be witness for me, with what gratitude I received my miraculous preservation! No longer the helpless victim of fell revenge, no longer crouching under the ruthless arm of a ruffian, I felt my afflictions no more: they vanished like a frightful dream, which the cheerful beams of morning had dissipated. And I now appeared as indeed a soldier, encompassed by a hardy band, in the gay trim of war, to which the rising light gave new lustre: still farther irritated by the black design of murder; loudly encouraging me to rely on their protection, and to bid defiance to the ungenerous cruel Count. Nor was this confidence slightly founded; for I learned that by their revolt Mal-leon was deprived of a force, which fully equalled all that yet remained under his command."

SECTION V

"They now marched on, publicly disclaiming all obedience but to their chief Les Roches; not as intending hostilities, but determined to retire from the island; and to demonstrate the sincerity of their declarations, the guards lately overpowered were already freed and courteously dismissed; nor was even the surviving ruffian detained. Count Savourè could not look with unconcern at so alarming a defection in his troops. All his remaining force was instantly collected, and soon were we confronted by a considerable body led by the proud Count, that stopped our farther progress: and while each party drew up in formidable array, each was possessed with anxiety and expectation. On our side, a firm resolution to support our purpose to the last, was unalterably fixed in every heart, yet with humane concern and generous reluctance against shedding the blood of countrymen, endeared by natural affection, and a long social intercourse. The little armies stood for a while in a state of sullen inaction louring upon each other: a delay which seemed to declare that neither presumed on any superiority, and that both expected, and desired a parley. This was at length proposed by my friend, and readily accepted.

"The commanders on each side advanced with a few attendants: and first Mal-leon proudly demanded the reason of this appearance of disloyalty and hostility. Les Roches repelled his accusation by recounting the injuries that had been offered to his honour and independence; urged the ungrateful returns made to his free and faithful services, by a vile unprovoked imprisonment, and declared that his sole purpose was to withdraw his arms from a Lord, who had loaded him with wrongs and disgrace. To this the Count replied, that the present appearance discovered clearly the necessity and the justice of his late conduct: that it now plainly appeared that Les Roches had united with his enemy and the enemy of his country, to tear the island from him; and that far from having oppressed or injured him, nothing but his own mistaken lenity had enabled a false Frenchman to proceed in this traitorous design. For this had he rescued from him the man who had basely stolen upon his territory, to corrupt his dependants, and to arm them against their Lord; for this he had murdered his officer, who gallantly opposed his unjust attempt; and for this he now stood in arms, ready to sacrifice his kinsmen and countrymen, to the treacherous purpose of an Englishman, who did not dare to meet him bravely in the field, but laboured to destroy him by the secret practices of fraud and circumvention.

"To this, my friend answered with a generous warmth, That as my soul was incapable of a base design, so my manner of coming into the island plainly removed all suspicions of any attempt against his government: that, cast as I was upon his shore, helpless and unattended by any numbers that could create the least fear, my endeavours had solely been exerted to elude his search, and to regain my native country: that all his own offence had been an endeavour, though fruitless, to favour the secret retreat of a noble enemy to whom he owed his life and liberty: nor could he repent of his grateful efforts, when no ransom was to be accepted, no captivity or restraint was deemed sufficiently severe, for a noble, generous, and unhappy Lord; when the ruffian had been hired to shed his blood, and in the dead hour of night dared to lift the murderous dagger against his unoffending, unsuspecting innocence.

"Suspicion, grief and indignation now raised a confused murmur among the attendants of Mal-leon; the same impressions, together with the story of intended murder, quickly reached their associates and spread contagiously through their lines; while the anguish of confusion, shame, revenge, and disappointment, turned the aspect of Count Savourè to ghastly pale. Yet, dreading the effects of this discovery, he soon endeavoured to assume a look of composure and conscious integrity; exclaimed loudly against the infamous contrivance to destroy his honour, and vehemently disavowed all intentions, but such as were fully warranted by the laws of honourable war. This declaration silenced the disorder in his troops; whose honest hearts could not without regret believe their general guilty of so black an attempt: he warmly repeated his professions of innocence; and called for the soldier said to be accomplice to him in whose breast Les Roches had plunged his sword. The steady villain now stood forth, and assumed such a countenance as effectually concealed his falsehood from every human eye. In the face of both the armies, falling upon his knees and lifting his eyes towards heaven, he called on every saint to bear witness to his innocence, and with horrid imprecations of the divine wrath, declared, that the only orders of his Lord had been to treat their prisoner with respect and care befitting an illustrious soldier. The constancy and the fair appearance of ingenuous sincerity which accompanied these solemn declarations, failed not of their desired effect: the troops of Count Mal-leon were fired with indignation, and joyed to find that their commander had not acted unworthy of his own and of his country's honour; they expressed a violent and tumultuous rage against the author of this supposed calumny; whilst the adherents of the good Les Roches were confounded and abased. Their eyes were turned upon me, with suspicion and cold distrust; the boldest among them ventured to break out into rude invectives, and to propose that I should be instantly delivered up into the hands of their brave countryman, whom I had so basely abused by my horrid imputations. My enemy exulted; my friend, though still amply satisfied of my truth and honour, was perplexed and grieved; and the fate of Salisbury seemed to depend on a single moment of tumult and confusion; when with an effort of desperate resolution I stepped forth, and while both parties hung upon me with looks of mute suspense and expectation, I recounted plainly and clearly all my adventures, since fortune had driven me to this unkind shore; my departure from the Abbey, with a full intention of resigning myself into the power of the Count, in order to preserve my friend: my being seized by the guards, and detained on the spot where they had found me, instead of being conducted to prison, or to the presence of Mal-leon; a circumstance full of suspicion! I described that dreadful night in all its horrors, when I had been so wonderfully delivered from instant death. And if any doubt remained of my truth and sincerity, I offered to make my solemn appeal to heaven. 'There!' said I, casting down my gage, 'I am ready to prove upon that recreant Lord his vile falsehoods, and to assert my own innocence, and his dishonour, in single combat.'

"Thou hast seen two gallant bands closing with each other; and for a while maintaining the conflict in terrible suspense, pressed and receding, recovering and pressing, by turns, until one mighty effort determines the fortune of the day, and the whole tumultuous rout of vanquished and victors, pour along the plain. Such had been the war of passions in these two parties, and such was now the force with which both were hurried away. My bold challenge was received with an unanimous acclamation by men too zealous votaries of warlike glory and honour, to desire, that baseness and falsehood should be supported or concealed. Shame forbade the Count to decline this hardy trial, and though appalled by conscious guilt, he accepted my defiance. Les Roches, whose friendly cares never were diverted from me, demanded an interval of two days to restore my harassed mind and body to their native vigour, and to prepare me for the encounter. This could not be refused: the time, the place, and every previous circumstance was soon adjusted as the laws of arms require; and each party drew off in silent expectation of the event.

"On the second morning, as I revolved my late dangers, and indulged the pleasing thoughts of my fate being soon to be decided by the fair and honourable chance of arms, an officer from Count Mal-leon appeared before the place of my residence and demanded admission to Lord Salisbury. I received him accompanied by my friend. 'Count Savourè,' said he, 'thirsts not for thy blood. It hath been thy desire to depart this island in peace: he commands me to acquaint thee that a barque is prepared, and that thou mayest, unopposed and unmolested, seek thy native land: he wishes not to detain thee, nor regards the honour of vanquishing Lord William as the least accession to his renown.' My eyes darted fiery indignation upon this messenger of abject fear. 'I defy his power,' said I, 'and scorn his friendship. I stay not here by his permission, and without his permission will I depart. Thinks he that an English Lord will sully his fair fame, and meanly steal away from honourable danger? Bear back my defiance to the man who should entertain so base a thought. Tell him I shall here wait, and wait with impatience for the dawning of tomorrow.' The officer departed: my friend embraced me with tears of joy, whilst I felt my heart cheerful and dilated; and from this overture derived an happy presage of victory.

"The morning of combat now appeared; nor did I wait the summons of my friends, but impatient for the great decision, I prevented their officious care and stood before them in arms, demanding to be conducted to the lists. These were prepared with every accustomed provision and defence against fraud or treachery. And while I entered on one side attended by Les Roches and his chosen companions, Count Savourè appeared with an equal number of attendants on the other, darting looks of deadly hate, rather than of manly valour. We advanced towards each other, not with the courtesy of honourable rivals, but sullen and indignant, silent and disdainful. Our assistants having first exacted the usual oaths, in which we disclaimed all unlawful methods of defence, all fraudulent or magical resources, separated us from each other, and pointed out our just stations. Here, while our horses pawed the ground, impatient to start forward, we waited the signal of the trumpets: when suddenly our attendants burst into the middle space, and called upon us to dismount. We obeyed; and as I advanced towards the crowd of knights and squires, I soon discovered my dear and reverend friend the Abbot, directing and commanding them with a paternal authority. Two were ordered to take charge of our horses and our weapons, whilst the father approached and invited us to a private conference. 'Lord Mal-leon,' said he, 'hear me, and tremble at thy presumption: tempt not the wrath of heaven, by exposing thyself to the hazard of arms in a cause which thou knowest is unjust. And do thou, Lord William, remember, that thou art forbidden to seek a brutal revenge.' The Count was just preparing to express his indignation at such a bold and unexpected interruption, when the father surveying him with a look of pity mixed with some degree of scorn, proceeded thus. 'The wretch hired by thee to shed the blood of this un-happy Lord, though sorely wounded by Les Roches, was yet left with some remains of life; the peasants bore him to our house for relief, and ghostly comfort. There he ex-pired; but not before his parting breath had publicly de-clared the dreadful purpose—but I will not wound thy ears with the horrid recital. Alas! thy shame is but too well known. If thou hast yet the smallest remains of goodness, dare not by this combat to defy the award of heaven: nor longer pursue this Lord with causeless hatred.' My rival now seemed to shrink before me, into all the meanness of disgrace, and abject baseness: whilst my triumph was more exalted, than the most successful event of combat could have given. My eyes were lighted up with indig-nation, but my heart disdained reproaches. Whilst I em-braced the reverend father, and freely submitted my arms to his direction and control, anguish, shame, remorse, and envy seemed to tear the soul of Mal-leon with their united tortures; tears burst from him, not the gentle drops of penitence; but tears of vexation, of disappointed and detected malice. Silent and trembling, he seemed irresolute for some moments: then, in sullen and broken accents, he just forced out: 'I will not—depart—I will not fight with thee—my prisoner—yet I seek no ransom: retire from this island; and henceforth avoid my fury.' Here a loud shout prevented my reply. The soldiers of Les Roches, by this time informed of the tidings which the Abbot brought, and which were no longer secret, hastened to receive me with their gratulations; and whilst they accompanied me to their camp, the base Count, followed by a silent and dejected party, marched away, and covered his disgraced head in the recesses of his castle."

Book II

SECTION I

The good old Knight could not suppress his exultation at the final issue of this dangerous contest. He pressed the hand of Lord William with an affectionate warmth, and congratulated him on his victory over his base and treacherous foe, a victory much more complete, much more mortifying to his rival, than could possibly have been acquired by arms. But the Earl soon restrained his joy, by acquainting him that this event did not put an end to his dangers. Randolph once more composed himself into a grave and earnest attention, and Lord William thus resumed the story of his fortunes.

"To retire from this odious scene of my calamity was now the great purpose upon which my soul was fixed. I had leisure to indulge my wishes to regain my friends, my country and my wife; and earnestly entreated Les Roches to crown all his goodness by speedily recalling my countrymen, and providing a vessel to convey us to the English shore. He expressed his surprise and concern at this request, he urged the danger of attempting a return without a force sufficient to defend me against an enemy who could not be a stranger to such a design, and whose deadly hate must prompt him to arrest me in my passage. 'No, my friend,' said he, 'attend us into France. South of the city of Poictiers my castle lies: at no inconvenient dis-

39

tance from the coast. Thither permit me to conduct thee: and thence with a retinue befitting his greatness, shall Earl William be attended in honour and security to England.'

"The apprehensions of falling once more into the hands of malice and insolent revenge, prevailed over my impatience, and determined me to embrace this friendly counsel. A few chosen followers were dispatched to Rochelle, where my countrymen lay in anxious expectation of their leader, who informed them of our fortunes, and after an interval of some days returned with all conveniences for transporting the forces of Les Roches. Our embarkation wore a gay and gallant aspect, conducted with cheerfulness and zeal, without fear of danger or control. The last vessel had now received my friend and me, and was on the point of leaving the shore; when we discovered a soldier hastening down towards us, and with extended arms entreating to be received. We demanded his name, and the reason of his extraordinary appearance. 'Alas!' cried he with that abasement which marks out calamity and oppression; 'but yesterday the officer of Mal-leon, favoured and honoured by my leader; now, the victim of his wild revenge, unless your protection shall deign to shield the unfortunate D'Aumont.' Here our attention was awakened, and I soon discovered that he was that messenger who the morning before our intended combat had accosted me with those overtures which fear had extorted from Mal-leon. As he stood upon the beach, with the passionate warmth of a sincere and deeply-pierced mind, the soldier thus proceeded: 'When insolent revenge and cruelty point their ungenerous fury against a valiant but unfortunate rival, what heart must not be moved; and what brave son of war can conceal his indignation? Let the coward dissemble his emotions: alas I have not learned his virtue, nor know I that mean reserve which he calls prudence. Lord

Salisbury is the enemy of Count Savourè, but a gallant and an honourable enemy. Let me ever emulate his exalted virtues, and scorn the base and cruel envy that would oppress them. We were soon no strangers to his fortunes; and while the abject minions of a proud Lord suppressed their pity, my thoughts were not so obedient to control; they forced their way boldly: and surprised my fellow soldiers with the most ardent expressions of indignation at the malice of our leader, whose flatterers treasured up the dangerous discourse, and failed not to convey it faithfully to his ear. And now D'Aumont was marked out for destruction: when rage and vengeance were ready to seize me; I fled. If my services may merit your protection, use them, and save me from ruin. Should Savourè spare and forgive me; witness, ye holy angels! this arm shall never draw its weapon for that dishonourable Lord. No! if I am abandoned, let me wander in disgraceful obscurity, let me feel the hard hand of want and poverty, or let me die rather than be made, perhaps, the minister of bloody cruelty on some brave soldier, who hath become odious by his virtues.'—Dangerous hypocrisy! how exactly canst thou assume the fairest semblances of goodness! O why should generous and ingenuous minds be more particularly the prey of thine accursed artifice?—We received him without the least difficulty or suspicion; and his wily arts of insinuation not only wrought us to pity, but soon commanded our affections and implicit confidence. On me his attention was perpetually engaged, ever officious in performing all the little offices which bespoke respect and love. His tears flowed instantly at the mention of my misfortunes; his eyes were lighted up with indignation, at the very name of my enemy. If we spoke of his cruelty, he trembled; if of his cowardice, he smiled with contempt, or frowned with stern abhorrence. In a word, the ardour of his affection seemed not so much the effect of humanity, as of a long, an intimate and tender friendship. Les Roches admired the virtues of this D'Aumont: nor could my heart refuse its full return of affection and gratitude to such exalted goodness. D'Aumont became our friend and counsellor: he shared our thoughts and directed our actions.

"We were now happily arrived at Rochelle, where I embraced my countrymen, whose suspense and apprehensions were at length dispelled. Filled with joy and gay expectations, we all advanced forward towards the domain of our kind protector, confident of comfort and security under his hospitable roof. His followers, no longer deeming their services necessary to their Lord, and impatient to revisit their several habitations, separated in their march; and left us, not wholly unattended, but at the head of an inconsiderable body, when we at length arrived at the castle of Les Roches. Here we had been taught to expect the cheerful welcome of affection; and here we now looked for joy and congratulation, the kind greetings of friends, and the officious cares of domestics. But alas! we had entered the mansion of sorrow. On every face sat silent grief and consternation, and chilled our souls with terrible apprehensions. My friend cast his eyes round with the most earnest anxiety; sometimes they turned on me; now on his attendants. At length he rushed precipitately from us, and traversed the apartments, as if in search of something particularly dear to him. I looked upon D'Aumont, who seemed equally astonished and equally uninformed of the cause of this strange disorder. Some few broken exclamations of surprise and solicitude were all that my tongue could utter. Tortured with expectation, and impatience to know the worst that fortune threatened, I eagerly waited the return of my friend, certain to receive the news of some calamity, but utterly incapable of forming the least conjecture of its nature, circumstances or extent. Les Roches prolonged his absence to a tedious and afflicting length. At last a domestic appeared, and called for D'Aumont; who, as he departed, turned upon me with a look of surprise and concern, then vanished, and left me to all the torture of uncertainty. A thousand extravagant conjectures did my fancy form, and reject by turns. My countrymen, equally perplexed and agitated, gazed on me and on each other in silent astonishment. 'Good heaven! what new wonders! for what are we reserved!' Thus did I exclaim; and in that moment some attendants entered, and with courteous and gentle demeanour inviting us to follow, conducted us to several chambers where refreshment was provided with all hospitable care; yet in all the silence and solemnity of sorrow. Thrice did I essay to speak my wonder, and as often did fear suppress my voice. Still my friend delayed his appearance: but after a tedious and distracting interval, D'Aumont at length stood before me, with an aspect which redoubled all that horror which my soul had for some time felt. I eagerly enquired about Les Roches; 'Alas,' said he, 'I know not what sudden gloom hath possessed this Baron. He hath long since departed with a few attendants: on me devolves the command of this castle. I am now his officer, and must implicitly obey his orders: and his orders are, that the Lord of Salisbury should be entertained with all honours: a prisoner indeed, but a noble prisoner, the rigours of his confinement must be duly allayed, by respect and careful attention.' I started, and exclaimed—'Prisoner! Confinement! Explain this wonder.' 'Such,' said he, 'are the commands of Les Roches. This chamber must content thee. The guards who are to confine thee within these bounds are enjoined the strictest vigilance, yet with due deference and care to do thee service.' 'Do I dream?' cried I, 'is this real? is this my hospitable reception?' Then pressing the hand of D'Aumont, whose dejected looks seemed to promise sympathy, and tender pity, I eagerly urged him to give me the whole story of this surprising change. Again indulging my distractions; 'Is Les Roches false to me?' said I. 'O no, it cannot be; the good, the tender, the affectionate Les Roches, my friend, my preserver? Do not wrong his virtues. It cannot be. Where is he? why delays he? O wretch, why dost thou torment my soul with idle terrors?'

"The Frenchman appeared violently moved at my disorder. His tears (for he could command tears) flowed freely; his sighs were deep and frequent; and his voice broken and interrupted: at length, as if recollecting some share of reason and calm reflection, 'Unhappy Lord!' said he, 'too truly have I declared thy situation. But what hath moved Les Roches to this, or for what fortunes Earl William is reserved, alas, is yet a secret to D'Aumont. Too true it is that some extraordinary event hath called away the Lord of this place. Perhaps he hath found it necessary to deliver thee back into the power of Mal-leon; perhaps he hath rescued thee from the rage of that proud Count, that he may have the glory of displaying to his countrymen an illustrious captive won by himself. But I fear his virtue most. Yes! it must be so. He hath indeed preserved thee from the treacherous attempts of base envy, but his duty to his Prince and to his country forbids him to restore to England the champion that hath fought her battles against France. O rigid sense of duty, that thus tears asunder the bands of nature and friendship. Happy D'Aumont, whose soul aspires not to such high unfeeling virtue! who cannot resist the tender solicitations of pity! Let me ever indulge the kind emotion, uncontrolled by rigorous scruples, or splendid notions of duty, too severe and too exalted for humanity.'

"These suggestions exactly answered to his purpose. My soul was too much disordered to examine them by the rules of calm deliberate reason; and the emotion which he assumed, increased my inward tumult, and gave him entire possession of my heart. In this fatal moment, the tenderness, the zeal, the solicitude, the sufferings of Les Roches all vanished from my thoughts. I had even forgotten the confusion which appeared in his castle on our arrival, and his own surprise and concern. I had forgotten that some unexpected event must have torn him from me. I imputed his absence to no other cause but the shame of encountering the looks and reproaches of a man whom he had betrayed: and all confused and distracted as I was, resigned myself entirely to the influence of this new friend, whose power was like that of those infernal imps who, they say, command the winds to roar or be still, and the waves to swell or to subside, as their wicked purposes require. As he depressed or roused me, I melted into grief, or raged in all the violence of vain and impotent indignation. I now considered myself as an helpless prey, doomed to inevitable destruction, surrounded on all sides by my hunters, and fatally lured to their toils. Nor was D'Aumont at all solicitous to dispel my fears. He expatiated on the horrors of a dungeon, on the wretchedness of captivity, the cruel tyranny of exasperated enemies and rivals, the loss of friends and honours; years of bondage spent in gloomy solitude, in useless inaction; the gazing curiosity of the base and ignoble, the insolence and triumphant scorn of the coward, who had perhaps trembled at my sword, and fled from my arm in battle: then, as if afraid to dwell upon the terrible idea, he just hinted at the tears of my friends, and the sorrows of an helpless widowed wife.

"Hast thou never heard that the enemy of mankind oftentimes presents shocking and frightful phantoms before the eyes of the holy hermit, in order to distract his thoughts and to confound his purposes? Such were the arts by which this Frenchman practised upon my soul. I started up in a sudden fit of fury and extravagance. I cursed my own blindness and folly, that had betrayed me into the power of my enemies; and when I had once escaped, had seduced me into France, instead of steering directly for the shore of England. Then madly seizing D'Aumont, I thundered out terrible execrations on his head, and wild menaces of vengeance, as an accomplice in cursed treachery. He trembled; and with silent looks and tears seemed kindly to reproach my unjust suspicions: then, in broken and imperfect words, appeared to struggle with his passions, and complained of the wrong done to his friendship. I instantly melted into all the tenderness of grief and affection: and ardently embracing the Frenchman, I acknowledged my error, and requested his assistance and council, in this my dangerous situation. 'Alas!' said he, 'if I am true to Salisbury, I must betray Les Roches. Hard situation for the soldier, who owes exact obedience to the dictates of duty and honour. But too well I feel that my heart is not secured against the assaults of pity. Yes, I am thine! and wholly thine!' Here he clasped me in his arms; and thus proceeded. 'I must deliver thee; and one moment's delay may deprive me of that power. Here we must not abide. Let us depart together; and let me share thy fortune. Some friends I have that shall receive and comfort thee. I know the way which leads to the coast, and will conduct thee. Thence may Lord Salisbury soon find means of returning to his native country: and thither (for thou wilt not leave me to the mercy of our common enemies) shall D'Aumont attend thee.' I heard him with eagerness, and implicit confidence. Without pause or reflection I submitted to his guidance; and in that very hour, we both departed from the castle."

SECTION II

"Thus had I rashly ventured forth into a wide and unknown scene of danger; under the direction of a false guide, whose treachery was soon discovered. It was night; and the moon cast her mild gleam over all the prospect that lay before us. D'Aumont repeated his assurances of friendship, spoke with cheerfulness and confidence, encouraging me to hope, and to fix my reliance on his services. I expected every instant to be conducted to some place of retirement and friendly reception. Sometimes I expressed my uneasiness, but ever and anon my guide practised his arts of soothing persuasion, and flattering professions, to allay my fears; thus we proceeded for some hours; at length, in our tedious progress, we passed by the skirts of a thick forest, from whence our ears were first pierced with shrill and lamentable shrieks as if from a female voice, and instantly afterwards, there issued out a small number of armed men, who surrounded us, and demanded our names and quality. My companion, nothing alarmed at this appearance, made the like enquiries on his part, and learned that they were the soldiers of Chauvigny Lord of Poictiers. 'I seek that Lord,' said he; when one of the soldiers surveying him attentively, replied, 'D'Aumont!—I know thee now! what from Count Mal-leon!' I started at the hideous name, and turning on my companion, perceived that the blood had deserted his cheeks, and that he stood in violent agitation. But ere I could express my wonder, retiring a few paces from me, he cried out: 'There stands Lord Salisbury: my purpose was to conduct him to Poictiers: he is now your prisoner, and let him be quickly conveyed to your Lord.' I stood confounded for a moment at this astonishing treachery, then quickly drawing my sword, I ran furiously upon D'Aumont; nor was it without the utmost difficulty that the soldiers restrained my just vengeance, overpowered, and disarmed me; then leading me into the wood, we joined some others of their body, who were intently engaged on a spectacle of pity.

"A youth who seemed just rising to manhood, of graceful form, tall of stature, and with limbs of perfect shape, lay sorely wounded upon the ground, languid, pale, and bloody. Over him hung one in the habit of a page, younger, and still more exquisitely beautiful, piercing the air with lamentations, and eagerly employed in binding up the wounds of the fallen youth, with locks of comely auburn, torn from a fair though dishevelled head. No sooner had the soldiers proclaimed my name to their associates, than the page, turning upon me with a face which discovered one of nature's most lovely productions, sullied and disordered by grief, just exclaimed: 'O fatal cause of all my misery!' then bending down again, as if disdaining attention to any but one favourite object, resumed the charitable cares of assisting, and supporting the wounded youth; who by this time revived from his trance, and cast a languid look of love and tenderness upon his kind companion. 'O Jacqueline,' said he, 'are we then prevented? But thou hast escaped the present danger. Nor shall force tear me from thee, or time efface thy remembrance.' This was answered with deep sighs and tender looks which spoke an affection ardent and powerful, though controlled by the presence of strangers. Every word and every action increased my surprise. Utterly unable to conceive how any part of the distress I now beheld could be imputed to me, I attempted with all courtesy to accost the page; who, on the other hand, had no eyes, no ear, no voice for me. But how was my astonished soul afflicted and confounded, when one of the soldiers casually discovered that this page was no other than a young maiden, and daughter to Les Roches! Whilst she was busily employed about the wounded youth, and with the assistance of some soldiers raising him from the ground, I turned to D'Aumont with looks of rage and anguish. 'Wretch!' said I, 'explain this wonder. Is this the work of thy cursed treachery?' 'No, proud Lord,' replied the false Frenchman. 'This youth is son to Count Chauvigny, whose prisoner I have made thee: but were he mine enemy, I am no murderer. Witness for me, that if my nature had been cruel, I might have plunged the dagger into thine own heart. What though I promised Mal-leon to use all my art to separate thee from thy protector, and to betray thee into the power of the Lord of Poictiers, yet I scorn the base work of blood! I have used my art, and with success: I have served my country and my chief, to whose hand the laws of war, and thy fate consign thee, and to whom thou shalt be soon restored by his friend Chauvigny.'

"I prepared to retort this insolence, when the soldiers interrupted, and commanded me to attend them to Poictiers: whither we now bent our course, the wounded youth being supported by the soldiers, and followed by the sorrowful Jacqueline. But scarcely had we proceeded a few paces, when another and a larger body of armed men was discovered, rushing precipitately across the plain. My guards nothing doubting but that these were friends, took no pains to avoid their approach. As they poured down upon us, their leader cast his eyes on me, and with plain marks of surprise pronounced my name, when instantly the whole party fell with the utmost fury upon my guards. They in vain endeavoured to support an unequal contest, encouraged by the voice and actions of D'Aumont, who fought with desperate rage. Impatient to take a share in this encounter, I suddenly snatched my sword from the soldier who had seized it, and flew upon my betrayer, but ere I could execute my just vengeance, his false heart was pierced by another arm. My guard were at length wholly overpowered: a few lay bleeding; the rest yielded their arms and were made prisoners, together with the wounded youth and his fair attendant, almost expiring with terror and astonishment.

"And now I learned from my deliverers some part of that distress, in which I had involved the good Les Roches, and the danger which I had escaped. Hear the story, as it was then, and afterwards unfolded, still more clearly. The delay of our embarkation from the Isle of Rhè had given the implacable Mal-leon an opportunity of dispatching a messenger to Lord Chauvigny, by whom he accused Les Roches of practices against his government, and of wresting from him a prisoner of so much consequence as Salisbury. This Lord, fired at the supposed injury offered to his friend, seized the castle of Les Roches, with the too common violence of a neighbouring and more powerful Baron; and carried off his only daughter, as a pledge for my surrender, if still in the hands of Les Roches, or as a means of awakening my sense of honour and gratitude, and thus obliging me to return, if already dismissed. Hence the grief and confusion of the domestics, at our arrival, and hence, the disorder of my friend: who, dreading my impetuosity, and well remembering how rashly I had resolved to deliver myself to Count Mal-leon, in order to gain his liberty, determined to conceal from me the cause of this disorder, and to try what might be effected by force of arms for the rescue of his daughter. D'Aumont, with whom he consulted, and to whom he spoke his fears of my precipitate generosity, commended his resolution; and as he prepared for immediate departure in order to collect his force, the false Frenchman proposed, that to himself should be committed the care of preventing me from leaving the castle, in his absence. How he abused this trust, thou hast already heard: but heaven was pleased to make his treachery the means of my preservation. Chauvigny who was still further informed of our approach, and of the weakness of our retinue, determined to make himself master both of mine, and of the person of my friend: and no sooner had I departed from the castle, under the conduct of my perfidious guide, than it was again seized by a force detached for that purpose, whilst another body hastening to support their associates, accidentally encountered Les Roches, dispersed his followers, and were only prevented from seizing him by the desperate valour of my seven Englishmen, whose attendance he had required, and who now with difficulty secured his retreat. A number of his followers thus dispersed, fled with precipitate haste towards their private haunts, for present security, and to collect new force for the deliverance of their chief; and in their flight, proved my deliverers.

"They now submitted to my direction, and invited me to share their fortune; and by my persuasion they dismissed the soldiers of Chauvigny, together with his wounded son. I embraced the youth at his departure, who seemed confounded and ashamed at the violence with which his father pursued a stranger thus superior to revenge. His eyes were turned on Jacqueline, whose looks and tears expressed all the anguish of separation. But the daughter of my dearest friend was a treasure not to be entrusted to the mercy of an enemy; and she was therefore detained however reluctant. My deliverers, anxious for our security, conveyed us with rapid speed to the fastness of an high and dreary mountain, where an humble cottage received, and the kind offices of honest poverty relieved us. And here, the maid, whose beauty created love and reverence in the breast of every beholder, informed me freely of her dangers and distress. Soon as she had been conveyed to the castle of Poictiers, the young Chauvigny already no stranger to the charms of Jacqueline, visited the fair prisoner, and endeavoured to allay her sorrows. Beauty, when distressed, is doubly powerful; and when pity unites with love, no heart can resist their impression. This the youth experienced. His soul became totally subdued; nor could he conceal the generous weakness. He pleaded, in all the most affecting accents of a sincere and ardent passion: nor did he plead in vain. The maid, too susceptible of tenderness, and too artless to conceal her sensibility, heard him with indulgence, approved his worth, nor frowned on his love. Yet still a greatness and elevation of soul, gave dignity to her female softness. She demanded a strong, and to a lover a severe, proof of his sincerity. 'Restore me to my father,' said she, 'then speak thy passion.' He entreated, wept, and conjured; she answered as before: till at length, the youth consented to the painful task of approving his sincerity, by parting with the dear object of his passion. A habit was provided to conceal the maid; and at the appointed hour, when guards had been bribed, and suspicion lulled to sleep, she issued forth, under the conduct of her lover, and directed her eager steps towards her father's castle. And fatal had been the end of this rash design, had not heaven wonderfully interposed. They had advanced considerably in their progress, filled with gay hopes, and insensible to danger, when some lawless rovers of the night, arrested, and began to rifle them. The young Lord patiently submitted to their depredations; but alarmed for his dear companion, and anxious to conceal the secret of her sex from brutal violence, he called upon them to spare the page, and with loud denunciations of vengeance, wildly assailed the wretch who was preparing to strip his Jacqueline. A sudden wound laid him on the earth; the forest echoed with the shrieks of the distracted maid; and in that moment the soldiers sent in pursuit of them (for their departure was not long concealed) happily appeared in view, and drove the robbers from their prey."

SECTION III

"I adored the preserving hand of heaven, whose influence had appeared so evidently in these events. The treachery of D'Aumont in seeking to destroy me, had opportunely conveyed me from the power of my enemies. The violence and oppression of Chauvigny, had proved the means of sending me deliverers, when fortune seemed most to frown upon me: and of giving up his own son to my mercy. I was now at liberty, if an obscure and comfortless retreat could deserve that name: I had delivered an helpless maid, the dear child and precious treasure of my friend, from the power of an oppressor: I was attended by honest and faithful followers, resolute to protect, and zealous to oblige me: yet still my soul was anxious for the fortune of the kind and generous Les Roches, whose virtues seemed to have drawn down ruin upon his injured head. Some emissaries I sent forth from time to time, to learn his fate: but no intelligence of his situation could be obtained. His castle was deserted, his friends dispersed, he himself lost in some obscure retirement with my gallant Englishmen, or perhaps slain by the malice of his pursuers. The proud Lord of Poictiers had in the name of his prince (unwarrantably assumed to support his oppression) proclaimed him a traitor; and denounced death against those who should presume to assist him. Such was the rage and malice of disappointed pride.

"I joined my tears with those of the charming Jacqueline at these afflicting tidings. Weeks and months passed away in the tortures of anxious uncertainty. Though careless of my own fate, yet I felt the tenderest concern for my dear charge; whom I conducted from one retreat to another, as the alarm of danger drove us forward, or the advice of our followers directed. My cares had now taught her to love me, as a parent and preserver: and the magnanimity which she discovered amidst all her dangers and difficulties, commanded my respect and admiration. She endured fatigue not only with cheerfulness, but joy: and as if from her infant years inured to poverty and hardships, she seemed to have retained no memory of the ease and softness of prosperity; nor did the tear ever start from her eye, but at the recollection of her father. A courage above her sex, and a surprising recollection and command of thought much beyond her years, never once deserted her, in the most trying moments: so that, whoever beheld her manly garb, and observed her determined spirit, must have supposed that I was attended by a youth, not yet initiated in arms, but eagerly ambitious to become a soldier, and impatient to enter on the course of gallant action and renown. She it was who first proposed the design of quitting these ignoble retreats, and endeavouring to find her father, now, when time had abated the ardour of our enemy's pursuit; and she too suggested the disguise which effectually concealed us from jealousy and malice. By the assistance of our faithful adherents, the habit of a Palmer was provided for each: and thus accoutred, we ventured forth from our retreat; I, the father; she, the blooming son; whilst a few zealous and humble friends, themselves disguised, watched our steps at some distance, and waited to repel our dangers. Long time we journeyed on, and often were we indebted to the kind offices of charity, undiscovered and unsuspected. Oftentimes have I gratified the curious peasant, whose hospitable door was opened for our reception, with the recital of hardy deeds achieved by his noble countrymen when the Christian powers united against the infidel: and oftentimes have I repeated my tale, to gain his confidence, and to lead him to some discoveries that might direct me to my friend. But never could we receive the least information of Les Roches, or of his fortunes. Oblivion seemed to have involved him in her gloomy shades, deserted, abandoned, and forgotten by his unkind, ungrateful countrymen; yet ever and anon, the remembrance of his goodness, and the thought of those calamities in which I had involved him, recurred to torment my soul: nor was the melancholy idea ever absent from the mind of Jacqueline.

"Our excursions were prolonged to a tedious and oppressing length. Sometimes the heavy hand of fatigue and languor pressed sore upon my dear companion, and called for all my care and tenderness: and these were again amply repaid, when the violent and complicated griefs that preyed upon my heart threatened me with some heavy malady. Thus wandering on, and wearied in a fruitless search, chance rather than our own determination led us to the sea coast, where the wide extended scene displayed before me, awakened all my eager wishes to revisit England. Oftentimes did I cast my eyes forward towards that seat of honour and security, and as oft, did they turn back on France, as if in search of my dear and injured friend. Not my own fortunes only were now the object of my thoughts: Jacqueline, the child of my preserver, the partner of his sorrows and his sufferings, demanded a share in my solicitude. I had still gold to bribe the sailor to convey us to a harbour of safety. I could not bear the thought of leaving this precious pledge of friendship to the care of poor and helpless followers; and yet my soul was pained, when I made an effort to persuade her to seek refuge in an unknown country, and to resign her last faint hopes of embracing a beloved parent. Here all my address was employed, and every flattering suggestion urged to quiet her anxiety. All our disappointed enquiries I converted into arguments of the caution and vigilance of Les Roches, which must have effectually concealed him from the malice of his pursuers. I spoke of my own influence in the English court, of the military power I could command: and conjured her to rest assured that nothing was wanting for his protection but my appearance in England: that there I could command authority and power sufficient to support his rights, and redress his injuries. Her great soul was animated with new vigour and resolution at the thoughts of redress: and with a firmness which would have done honour to the bolder sex, she freely consented to submit to my direction, and declared herself ready to attend me.

"Our two followers, whose unwearied zeal had not yet lost sight of us, were now employed to procure a vessel to convey us from the land of danger and oppression: as two pilgrims, engaged by solemn vows to visit the lately erected shrine of St. Thomas of Canterbury; the fame of which had not been confined to England. Some days passed in expectation of their success, an interval which was employed in comforting my fair charge, and confirming her resolution. On the morning of a vernal day, we wandered forth from the charitable cottage, that lately had received us, to indulge our gentle conference without fear or control. The sun was climbing to his meridian height, and warned us to repose under the shade of a steeply rising hill, whose trees nodded over us, and embrowned the neighbouring plain. Here we had not long reclined, when the noise of jocund mirth struck our ears, and called our attention to two travellers, who lay at some distance, sharing their friendly meal. I started, and listened to the well known sounds; I heard my own native lays, sweetly rehearsing the renowned deeds of Arthur valiant prince, the ancient wars of Ambrose the Armoric knight, and the triumphs of British valour. I melted into tears, (such are the tender emotions which the love of country raises in our breasts) then rushing impetuously towards the travellers, I gazed on them with astonishment; they sprung from the ground, no less surprised, and I embraced two of my dear countrymen, and late companions. They surveyed me with joy and wonder, they acquainted me that their fellows were at hand; they asked by what miracle I had been preserved; but I at once stopped their enquiries by demanding to know the fate of Les Roches. Their cold and mournful looks at the mention of this name, chilled the blood of Jacqueline, who had by this time joined us. 'Say,' said she, in breathless agitation, 'when, how, where did Les Roches perish? Could not his followers defend him? Or did they desert him? Perfidious men! Where were their coward swords, when the malice of his persecutors tore his poor helpless body? No faithful friend to defend him? No charitable hand to close his dying eyes?' Here a flood of tears broke forth, while my countrymen wondered at her emotion: and eager to remove her suspicions declared, that Les Roches had wanted neither fidelity nor courage to defend him. 'Lives he?' cried the maid; 'where? lead me to him!' And again resigned herself to sorrow, when the Englishmen declared that they were strangers to his fate, nor knew his place of residence if yet alive. I interposed to moderate her passion; then turning to my friends, demanded the full relation of their fortunes, since treachery and oppression had last torn us from each other.

"They had been persuaded, (as I now learned) that I must have been seized in the castle, and that I now lay under the severe oppression of captivity; as Les Roches had instantly acquainted them with the secret of his daughter's being conveyed to Poictiers, with his apprehensions of my precipitate zeal, and the measures he had taken to prevent any rash purposes of throwing myself into the hands of my pursuers. They had attended him in his sudden excursion to collect his forces, and in the gallant act of defending him, they had been particularly animated by Fitz-Alan, the man whose inconsiderate error had first disclosed my name in the Isle of Rhè, and who now fought with redoubled fury, to atone for his fatal imprudence. He it was who, when Les Roches lay surrounded and disarmed, hewed his way through unequal numbers, and led the brave Englishmen to his rescue. They took their course from his direction, and conveyed him to the neighbouring hills, where secret and unvisited retreats received him, and where the vigilance and bravery of his followers guarded against the approach of fraud and violence. His own countrymen, awed by the denunciations of Chauvigny, deserted their unhappy chief, the helpless and abandoned victim of fatigue and want. The woods supplied his nourishment; the naked turf received his devoted head, whilst the fidelity and affection of his associates watched his broken slumbers. Long time had they attended him from one retreat to another, through a series of uniform distress, without any new or extraordinary change of fortune; 'till on one fatal morning, they whose industry had been employed in hunting for food, and they who had the charge of watching near his humble couch, were struck with confusion and surprise, when they came to seek their leader. He had suddenly disappeared, nor could their most diligent enquiries learn his new residence, or inform them of his fate. And now, impatient of their situation, and determined rather to yield themselves into the hands of their

enemies, than to waste a tedious life in distressful and useless retirement, they descended from their mountains, and
boldly adventured into more known and more frequented
paths. Here they soon found that the hopes of regaining
England were not yet to be resigned. Pursuit and difficulty had ceased: they passed on unnoticed and unmolested,
and at length gained the coast, where we were now all
happily assembled.

"The vessel lay ready to receive us; we embarked with
joy; yet still cautious to guard against malice and hostility,
I continued my disguise. The winds were long unfavour-
able; and frequently were our souls terrified with the most
alarming menaces of destruction. Twice did I embrace my
lovely charge, in firm persuasion that I had taken my last
and final farewell; and that the approaching hour must
have consigned us to one general ruin. Yet still the holy
saints denied not their protection. Courage and vigour unabated, successfully contended against the angry elements.
Harassed, wasted, and oppressed with toil, we at length
gained the cheering prospect of our dear native shore. Here
our shattered vessel happily arrived; and here we repose our
wearied limbs under your hospitable protection."

SECTION IV

The Earl ceased; and Randolph, who had listened with exact attention, paused for a moment, in thoughtful silence,
raised his eyes and hands to heaven, in rapturous admiration, and grateful acknowledgement of that power which
had hitherto conducted his friend safely through this vari-
ety of peril and distress; then freely exclaimed at the envy
of Mal-leon, the tyranny of Chauvigny, and the treachery
of D'Aumont, with all the zeal of generous indignation
and abhorrence. His tears confessed that pity with which

he thought on the cruel fate of Les Roches, and infected the Earl with a tender emotion of grief for the misfortunes of his dear friend and protector. He had not entertained the least suspicion but that his own misfortunes were now completely ended; that any thing more remained, but to repair to his castle, and comfort his solitary Countess; yet now, when restored to a degree of tranquillity, he again offered at some enquiries on his part, of his house, his son and wife, but was instantly interrupted by Randolph, who reminded him of rest. The night was far spent: fatigue and sleep, which the agitation raised by the recital of his adventures had hitherto repelled, now resumed their power, and invaded him with double force. He retired, and at last enjoyed the comfort (to him long unknown) of peaceful and secure repose.

Age had made Randolph watchful. He rose before the dawn; and was soon joined by the attendants of Lord William, who advanced to greet their host, and to acknowledge his generous cares. Their mutual salutations were cordial, and affectionate; the Englishmen seemed to have forgot their toils: lusty and spirited they stood accoutred, and prepared to meet their leader, earnest to tender their services, and impatient to accompany his progress. Nor did they long wait for the appearance of Lord William. He had sprung from his couch refreshed and restored to life and vigour, and now came forth to embrace the companions of his labours, and to repeat his congratulations. "My friends," said Randolph, "bear with us for a moment. I have something which demands the private attention of the Earl.—Yet—no—It need not be concealed from you. Your counsels may assist us." Thus speaking, he led the way towards a private apartment, whither he was followed by the Earl and his companions, not without some degree of wonder and anxious expectation.

Randolph cast his eyes downwards for some moments, and was silent: then turning them on Lord William, "For what fortunes," said he, "this Earl is preserved, I know not: but tranquillity seems yet to be removed to some distance from his grasp: something still remains to exercise his spirit. Raymond, nephew to that Hubert whose councils govern our King, now possesses his castle. There, and through all its district, he governs with an absolute sway."—"What!" cried Salisbury, "is my power expired! Do I indeed live? Or have my rights been forfeited?—Where were my friends? Hath my Countess been ignominiously driven out by the usurper? Is this the reward of my services?"—Randolph here repressed his violence: and demanding a calm and patient attention, the Knight thus proceeded.

"We all know with what uncontrolled power Hubert rules in the court of England: how his subtle arts of insinuation have penetrated into the inmost heart of our Henry; and now direct all its motions and designs. Already too dangerous, he seeks but to extend his influence and authority, and to heap wealth and honours on his family and dependants. These are his great purposes; and to these he sacrifices the reputation of his master, and the welfare of his country. To him was soon conveyed the false intelligence, that Earl William and his Knights, separated from our fleet in the tempestuous tumult, had perished in the deep. The King heard the tidings with kind concern, and paid the just tribute of sorrow to his unhappy kinsman, and brave soldier. The crafty Hubert assumed the semblance of grief, whilst his soul was busy in contriving the means of turning this event to his own interested purposes. He seized the easy and complying moment, when the King lay most open to his influence: he represented the close alliance, in which Raymond his good nephew stood to the illustrious house of Salisbury: he reminded him, that by the royal bounty, Lord William had obtained the heiress of that house with her possessions, and urged that the same royal bounty ought now to confer this gift on him, whom nature seemed to point out as the true inheritor. In a word, he asked this boon, that Raymond should be permitted to wed the Countess, now supposed a widow, and to enjoy her ample fortunes and her honours."—"Heavens!" exclaimed the Earl, "this man admitted to her bed!—Am I so soon forgotten? What? not a few months of sorrow!"—"Think not hardly of the Countess," said Randolph; "her dignity of soul!"—"Yes!" cried William again interrupting him, "I know it.—It cannot be—proceed, and give me all those strange events."—"The King," replied Randolph, "granted his suit without difficulty. 'Go,' said he, 'command Raymond to prepare for his departure: let him summon all his address and eloquence, to prevail upon the gentle Countess. No easy conquest, she; no common prize! My grace waits on her consent.' "—"Consent! impossible!" cried Salisbury; when Randolph again endeavouring to allay the heat of his impatience, earnestly united his entreaties with those of the Earl's companions, and at length obtained a patient audience.

"Raymond," thus the old Knight proceeded, "was not slow to accept this gracious condescension to his wishes. Supported by the power of Hubert, enriched by his bounty, and attended by the flattering followers of his prosperity, this Lord soon prepared all necessaries for a magnificent and stately progress. He left the English court, which now graced the city of Marlborough with its residence (for thither the indisposition of our liege had caused it to be transferred) and at the head of a gallant troop of Knights, armed, and caparisoned in all their courtly pride and splendour, and implicitly obedient to their leader, he proceeded towards the castle of Salisbury. The humble villagers gazed on this gay troop, with surprise and pleasure, were soon informed of their purpose, and soon spread the story through all the neighbouring land. The Countess had already learned the melancholy tidings of her Lord; and indulged her griefs in secret: when, roused by the appearance of this retinue, and nothing suspecting the purpose of Raymond, she opened her gates wide to his approach, and received him and his attendants with all hospitable rites, befitting her own nobility, and the greatness of her guests. To Raymond she appeared in all the dignity of grief, holding her young son, a fair copy of her beauty and her sorrow. And (if fame speaks true) the charms of the majestic mourner, had, in that moment, too powerful an influence upon the heart of Raymond. Love came in aid of his ambition, and inflamed the ardour of his pursuit. With all those soothing arts, which courts and their polished converse had bestowed, he laboured to dispel her gloom, and cautiously to introduce the great purpose of his arrival. Long time he suspended his declaration: (such is the controlling power of beauty surrounded by the aweful beams of chaste and graceful dignity) yet in every interview was his passion confirmed and increased. At length (so have we been informed) he spoke his suit with humble and anxious hesitation; and was received with surprise and scornful denial."

Whilst the Knight thus spake, a succession of violent passions had distracted the mind of Lord William. His eyes first expressed an earnest and tumultuous impatience. He trembled; and the blood retired from his cheeks; then rushed back to resume its seat, with double force, and glowed with fiery indignation. Again, his tender looks declared, with what love and gratitude and sympathising pity, he felt the sorrows of his beloved Countess. Impatience and anxiety again succeeded; and when the Knight paused, his looks had grown great, and elevated, and a sudden exclamation of triumph broke involuntarily from his lips. "What remains," said he, "but that we now go and resume our authority? What is wanting but our presence to relieve our Countess from this importunate wooer? Come, my friends! let us haste away. Let us break through that cloud of obscurity which hath too long concealed us; and confound the men who grasp at our rights and honours, with such a precipitate and rash presumption. Shall Ela weep, and I delay to comfort her? Shall proud intrusion break upon her privacy, and irritate her grief, and do I not fly to relieve her?" "Beware," replied the Knight with looks of sage and rigid caution, "beware of violence! consult not with thy passions. Thy Countess hath, I hope, maintained her firmness and constant purpose to the last. Should she—but I cannot fear it.—Yet still Raymond is in possession of thy castle; he acts as Lord of thy land and inheritor of thy power. Canst thou behold this usurpation calm and unmoved? Trust me, I dread thy impetuous resentment. Raymond is proud and insolent; Hubert crafty, dark, and revengeful. The injurious never can forgive. Shame and disappointment may drive him to desperate resolutions.—Alas, I cannot speak half my fears."

The mysterious language of the Knight, who, however he suppressed his fear, really dreaded a fatal compliance in the Countess, and formed the most terrible presages of broils and blood, kindled up a sudden flame in the breast of Salisbury. "Heavens!" cried he, "if Raymond should have already—I see the danger of my situation.—But let us quickly seek this invader." Randolph now seemed to condemn his own apprehensions, which he observed might arise from doubtful or mistaken information. His retirement had rendered him the more liable to be deceived; and despair of ever seeing the return of his friend had made him less solicitous in his enquiries. However, he still urged caution and calm procedure. He advised that some friends should be sent forward to the castle to declare the approach of Earl William. "This," said he, "will give an opportunity to Raymond to retire, without the shame of encountering the severity of his aspect, who comes to drive him from his usurped state, and without provoking thee to some rash deed of ungoverned passion. Then shall we follow; and peace, joy, and conjugal affection shall receive thee." The Earl approved his counsel; and consented to the desires of his companions, who pressed to be the harbingers of his approach. They instantly took their way: whilst Randolph dispatched his messengers to summon such a number of dependants as might afford an honourable conduct to the Earl, together with the fair Jacqueline, who now came forth, not in her disguise; but in a female garb, though not magnificent, yet better suited to display her modest graces, and to give new lustre to her beauty. It was resolved that for a few days they should continue with the hospitable Knight; an interval tedious and distracting to the Earl, whose mind was filled with doubts and fears; impatient to know more than had already been received from the imperfect intelligence of his host, yet dreading to hear something which might fatally wound his peace.

Book III

SECTION I

Whatever sadly-boding thoughts were entertained by Lord William, little did they correspond with that weight of anguish, which, by this time, had oppressed his wife; in whose castle, the insolence and cruelty of Raymond and his creatures had taken their lawless course, free from control. His first appearance had been courteous and gentle, befitting a noble visitant: nor did he disclose his purpose till he had gained the fair opinion of the unsuspecting Countess. Love and wedlock, when first made his theme, sounded like notes jarring and discordant, to the ear exactly tuned to harmony: and when he urged his suit directly, a sudden flood of tears confessed her inward emotion, such tears as indignation and disdain force from the eyes of distressed greatness, and high-born pride. Raymond stood amazed: and vain were his repeated endeavours to compose her disorder. At length, her passions thus found an utterance: "And dost thou know me? Hast thou ever heard that the greatness of soul which hath invariably distinguished my long train of mighty ancestry, is lost in me?—One year hath not yet elapsed, since these arms embraced my honoured lord. But had the grave long since received him; had time dried up my widow's tears, thinkest thou that the widow of a Plantagenet—But why talk I thus?—How knowest thou? What officious babbling slave hath flattered thee with the lying story that Lord William lives no longer; that the great light of England is extinguished, and that Raymond may now rise and shine?—It is false—I will not think it. Yet, yet will I hope for his return. Should he find thee here, (and this thy purpose!) what could defend Lord Raymond from his resentment? Thou knowest the mighty spirit of Earl William. Fly this moment; and tempt not thy fate. Nay, never frown! How would one single glance of his princely eye confound that haughty confidence? Know, presuming lord, that the slightest probability of his appearance should strike thee with terror." Thus saying, she turned scornfully away; lovely even in her disdain; and suddenly left her suitor in wonder and confusion: who, too deeply affected by her beauty, to submit to this repulse, solicited, entreated, and at length rather forced, than was admitted to a second interview. Earnestly did he urge his love, and with all the gentle eloquence of a sincere and ardent passion. Just to the deserts of Earl William, he acknowledged his high worth, and his own inferior merit: but the hopes of his return, he treated as desperate and unreasonable, and exerted all his art to banish from her thoughts the memory of a man, whom fate had long since buried in eternal oblivion.—"Behold this boy!" said the Countess, clasping her young son: "in him, at least, Salisbury still lives. And never can his mourning wife resign the dear melancholy remembrance of his greatness, while this precious pledge of former love, this lively image of a noble and honourable father, remains to soothe her sorrow. Behold him! see how all the princely dignity of William already sits displayed in his youthful front: and wonder not that Ela never can descend to any other passion."

Thus obstinate and inexorable, the Countess ever added scorn and reproof to her denial; insulted the love, and stung the pride of Raymond; whose disgrace was soon no secret to his attendants. Of these, the first, and principal in his confidence, was a man nurtured in courts; long practised in the arts of flattery, and the homage of dependence; trained to watch the looks, the smiles, the frowns of a superior, to aid his pleasures, to indulge his passions, to love, to hate, as he directed, with an obsequiousness equalled only by the insolence and oppression which he dealt out with unfeeling severity to all beneath him. Subtle and expert he was in the arts of fraud and circumvention; ever attentive to his own private interest; patient, persevering, and sagacious in the means of advancing it. His name was Grey. To him Raymond unbosomed his disordered thoughts; lamented his despised love, and the unrelenting pride of Ela, which threatened to blast all his hopes of ambition. The flatterer expressed the utmost indignation; and as if the resolution of the Countess had been unwarranted and injurious, injurious to the honour and dignity of Raymond, he censured him with an artful semblance of sincerity and zeal, as if he himself had been the cause of his own repulse: He accused him of indulging the perverseness and pride of this high dame, by the humble and abject strain of his addresses. He persuaded him that in this place he was now absolute lord and inheritor, who should command, and not entreat, graced as he was by the royal favour, and supported by the power of Hubert. The slightest hint was more than sufficient to inflame the pride of Raymond. He yielded entirely to the pleasing delusion, and already fancied himself undoubted heir of the house of Salisbury, and master of its ample domain. The conditions on which the King had assented to his petition, were totally forgotten: and he now determined to act agreeably to that high character, in which his imagination had arrayed him, and to extort that compliance to his wishes, which his solicitations could not obtain. Every thing was disposed at his command; and the domestics and inhabitants of the castle taught to acknowledge a new lord. To the Countess, he affected to appear, not as a humble lover, but an imperious sovereign master. Yet, awed by her dignity and beauty, he acted this part, not without constraint and shame; and still repulsed, and still despised, he required all the artifice and flattery of Grey, to support him in his purpose. Yet, this extraordinary change could not fail to alarm the fears of the Countess. With surprise and helpless indignation she found herself the prisoner of her guest. Her usual attendants were removed; and new domestics assigned, the creatures of her enemy, who performed the due offices to her and to her infant son, not with respect and care, but with sullen silence and reserve: and all her words and actions were free to the observation of strange and unfriendly keepers. If Raymond ventured to appear in her presence, (for still he dreaded the severity of her frown) with wild dismay, yet with the dignity of injured greatness, she demanded an explanation of this mysterious conduct: whilst he only urged the necessity of an absolute compliance with his desires, and left her agitated soul to divine the fatal consequences of a refusal. Sometimes she endeavoured to expostulate; to speak her wrongs boldly, and to menace her oppressors; but tears never failed to betray her inward terror, and to discover a lively sense of the weakness of her widowed state. Sometimes she called upon Lord William, and tormented herself with the remembrance of the virtues and renown of her lost protector. Sometimes she pressed her son with an eager and passionate fondness to her heart, and invoked every saint in heaven to save the precious creature. For him much more anxious, than for her own fate, she formed a thousand visionary schemes to rescue him from the oppressor; which, like fantastical dreams, vanished, and left her to despair. Raymond, though insolent and cruel, yet still loved the unhappy Countess; nor could he behold her distress without some pangs of remorse. But his unrelenting minion was ever at hand, to condemn and deride his weakness, (so he deemed it) and to persuade him that nothing but rigid authority and severe restraint could prevail upon the high mind of Ela, and reduce her to what his abandoned flattery presumed to call a reasonable compliance. Thus was her resolution still assailed, and still unconquered.

But greater trials remained for this unhappy lady. Grey, whose mind was not discomposed by passion, and who thought more coolly than his lord, seriously reflected on the necessity of forcing the Countess to give her hand to Raymond, in order to establish his rightful claim to an inheritance, which promised ample advantages to his creatures. And when the prospect of riches and rewards were presented to his view, his rapacious soul instantly became deaf to all the calls of pity; nor was one sentiment of humanity suffered to intrude upon his mind. The enamoured Raymond grew more and more impatient; and every hour lamented the inflexible spirit of the Countess, and her unalterable aversion to his love. His flatterer still wore a face of friendly anxiety and concern; and, as if he lived only for his lord, seemed to feel the disappointment as his own misfortune: and expressed that earnestness for conquering this difficulty, with which men generally pursue their private interests. Raymond was charmed with this specious show of zeal and sincere affection. He called him friend, guardian, and director; he lavishly promised wealth and honours; and entreated him to devise some means of accomplishing his wishes. Grey seemed for a while immersed in thought: then, as if suddenly recollecting himself, he assumed a look of confidence and exultation. "It cannot be!" thus he exclaimed: "This imperious Countess cannot forever prove insensible to the inviting voice of joy and happiness. She sees thy passion; and would inflame it by this affected delay. Or if her haughty soul be really unmoved, something must be thought of—Raymond must—yes, my ever-honoured lord, thou shalt possess her. Let me be favoured with thy confidence: submit to my direction. For some days shun her presence, for there thy weakness is discovered. Rely on my services; and let it be my part to prevail upon her."—"Go," said Raymond; "to you and to your conduct I implicitly resign my hopes. Prevail, and be great as thou canst wish."—Thus was the afflicted Countess given up to the hands of insolence and cruelty, without help or friend, without counsel or resource.

Instead of the man whose arrogance was tempered by that reverence and love with which her beauty had inspired him, Ela saw now before her an unrelenting, unfeeling vassal; in condition, such as her soul disdained to hold converse with, and in temper base and brutal. He approached her with a rude insensibility to her state, and to her sorrows. Instead of pleading the passion, or the merits of his master, he proudly demanded her compliance. He called upon her to consider his power, and her own condition: that she was no longer mistress in this stately castle, which, with all its wide extended lands, had devolved to Raymond; now the master even of her and of her son; and that she had only to choose whether to appear as his consort, in all the lustre that riches and royal favour can bestow, or to waste her solitary days in grief and abject dependence.

The Countess, though pierced with sorrow, and sensible of her helpless condition, surveyed the rude minion in disdainful silence. He repeated his bold remonstrances;

yet nothing more could his importunities extort than a stern command to retire from her presence. He obeyed; but soon returned, and repeated his odious insolence. In that moment her young son appeared, and flew with eager and fond caresses to his mother. At sight of him, she instantly forgot her greatness: her griefs burst forth in a sudden and violent stream. She embraced him with trembling arms: and the boy, though unable to conceive the cause, sympathised passionately with the Countess. The sight was pitiful and affecting; but the hardened Grey felt only a short and transient surprise. "Is he thus dear!" said he: "know then, that his mother's obstinacy may prove fatal to her son. The charge of him now belongs to Raymond. He best knows how to defeat all future attempts to dispossess him of his rights."—The Countess started up in speechless amazement: and Grey turned from her with a sullen menace, that henceforward her son should be a stranger to her arms. "Stay!" replied the Countess, pale and trembling with terror and virtuous anger; "hear me, cruel man—Heavens! is it for this that we are made prisoners within our own walls; shut up from society and relief? no access for comfort or friendship; no resource, no support for our helpless innocence? And did the bloody purpose of a murderer lurk beneath his courtly smiles, when Lord Raymond first entered our castle? And dreads he not vengeance? Have the friends of William all perished with him?—At least Heaven is our friend; and will repay the cruel deed. O! there is a blessed angel ever ready to present the cries of infant innocence before the throne of justice, and to implore for vengeance on the arm that hath been lifted against it—Seeks he our love? Mistaken lord! little dost thou conceive the fatal consequences of extorting a feigned consent, when the heart is still estranged. Cold indifference, distaste, aversion, and loathing, ever watch round the bridal bed, and fright away all joy and social comforts.—Seeks he our possessions?—Take them! enjoy them freely! and let us retire to some seat of humble obscurity; where no curious eye shall ever pierce through our recess; where the name of Salisbury was never known or uttered by the voice of Fame. There shall my child labour with the lowly peasant: and never shall his mother betray the secret of his birth. But if his blood must be the horrid purchase—O let Raymond secure his power and riches beyond the reach of time or fortune. Let me too perish. Drive not all mercy from your hearts: but spare me the dreadful sight of my child's blood. No! let me be made the first victim of your cruelty."

Pity and humanity for a moment assailed the ruthless heart of Grey; but soon were they repelled. He sternly answered, that she and her son might yet be happy; that the conditions were easy and honourable: but that disdain and pride were no good proofs of a mother's tenderness: that the fortune of this boy was in her power, and that, should he suffer, she herself would be the author of his sufferings.—Then calling the attendants, he commanded them to remove young William. His mother fell upon her knees, stretching out her trembling arms in expressive silence: To her bosom the boy fled for refuge from his infant terrors; she rose, and clasped him to her breast, devouring the dear object with eyes of frantic fondness. The ministers of cruelty relented and hesitated: but Grey severely repeated his command. They surrounded the distracted mother and her weeping son; soon conquered her feeble efforts to detain him, and tore him from her struggling grasp. Her shrieks echoed through the castle, and wounded the affrighted ear: till nature, harassed and exhausted by contending with the vast affliction, lost its powers, and the Countess lay pale and lifeless upon the ground. The tumult in her apartment had already reached the ear of Raymond, who flew to enquire the cause, and now came to be a witness of her distress. He soon learned the cause, and far from approving the cruelty of his minion, he received him with frowns and reproof. He ordered the female attendants to convey their afflicted lady to her couch, and with all tender cares to recall her dying senses. Thither he himself soon followed, to restore her dear son, and to calm her terrors: but she had now no ear for comfort. The fever had already seized upon her; inflamed her eye, and raged in her boiling veins. Her disordered fancy tormented her with killing images of terror; and his presence added new force to her delirium. Raymond felt all the violence of love and distraction: and Grey stood aghast. This subtle minion laboured, first, to appease the resentment of his lord, and then to give him comfort. He himself appeared most solicitous for the recovery of the Countess, although his wicked heart secretly exulted in her present danger. Should she live, and at length consent to accept of Raymond for a husband, his insolence must then be remembered, and his lord taught to detest the author of her sufferings. Should she still refuse to give her hand to Raymond, this lord could not long continue his oppression, but must soon resign his unjust pretensions, and thus dash all his own hopes of rich rewards. Nay, possibly his conduct might hereafter meet a severe punishment. Thus he reasoned: and regarded her death as an event highly to be wished. An infant heir might easily be disposed of, and Raymond invested with his rights without control or opposition. Every hour flattered his hopes with desperate accounts of Ela and her alarming situation. His art was exerted to the utmost, to divert the attention of Raymond from her distress, to alienate his mind from a woman who had presumptuously insulted his passion; and to dazzle him with the gay view of those fortunes which were now ready to crown his wishes. To inflame the pride of this lord, was his artifice and flattery principally directed. And, when he had warmed his imagination with prospects of riches and magnificence; when he had worked up his pliant mind to the due pitch of insolence and fierceness, he even dared to hint at the necessity of defeating all future claims; and with hardened calmness and indifference declared, that it must be his own care prudently and secretly to dispose of young William. Nor did Raymond, in his present temper, hear him with abhorrence or emotion. To such inconsistencies is the mind of man hurried by the tyranny of passions. He had just expressed the tenderest pity for the Countess; and now, when the determined villain had proposed to destroy her infant son, he started not at the horrid counsel, nor refused his consent.

SECTION II

But that pity which pride and interested cruelty denied her, Ela now found in her own sex. Her principal female attendant, though the creature of Raymond, and by him appointed for her service, had long beheld her sorrows and maternal fondness, with secret grief and sympathy. She had, herself, been wife and mother, had felt and known their endearments and cares. Long had she wept in secret for the afflictions of her injured lady, and now attended on her sick couch, with all the fond zeal and concern, which a woman's distress could excite in the gentle and feeling mind of woman. Her affection was now undissembled (for her Lord enjoined the most assiduous care, when the disorder had first seized the Countess,) and that affection was attended with success, proportioned to its ardour and sincerity. Nor time nor fatigue could abate her diligence and kind attention to a beloved mistress, who long lay insensible of her goodness, shrinking timorously from the hand that presented relief. At length, however, nature appeared still unconquered in this severe conflict. Reason began gradually to regain its native seat, and the Countess was restored to some composure. Elinor (so was her attendant called) watched the happy moment when she began to survey the objects round her without distraction, to offer comfort and consolation. She presented her son, who stood weeping by her side, to assure her of his security; and every office which duty and charity could dictate, she busily performed, to allay the violence of her malady, and to restore her languid spirit. The Countess, touched with her goodness, repaid her with the warmest expressions of regard and gratitude. Their affection was now mutual, and was succeeded by mutual confidence. Thus, even amongst its enemies, did oppressed virtue so far prevail, as to reconcile one mind, and to attach one relenting heart, to its injured cause. Ela every hour experienced the happy effects of tender care. She had recovered some degree of ease and strength: she had leisure to reflect upon her danger and difficulties: misfortune and solitude had effaced the proud thoughts of rank and greatness: and without reserve she opened her soul to this attendant; bitterly lamenting the severity of her fate; who, though she numbered many and powerful friends, though her fortune and condition gave her the command of a formidable band of vassals, yet by foul treachery was cut off from all relief, from all possibility of complaining, or petitioning for deliverance, subjected to the will of insolent and cruel enemies, and exposed to all the distresses of captivity, in that very place, where she was rightful mistress: strange reward for the services of her great father, and her noble husband!

The attendant, with ardent prayers, and lively effusions of pity and tenderness, gave her some slight consolation; but though she felt for her distress, she seemed incapable of devising any reasonable means of relief. Hope, patience, and such like terms, which sound but harshly in the ear of affliction, she repeated with a warm but impotent zeal; she even ventured to hint at the expediency of assuming an appearance of less severity to Lord Raymond; of flattering his fond expectations for a while: thus, to amuse the busy and contriving malice of his creature, to gain some interval of ease, some happy respite from persecution. Time and the interposition of heaven might then work wonderfully for her deliverance. But the soul of Ela still retained a dignity superior to the arts of dissimulation. She started with abhorrence, at the thought of sullying her bright fame by any suspicious conduct, any semblance of unworthy condescension. Her high mind dwelt with more pleasure on the flattering thoughts of redress and vengeance. She reflected that the land still contained many powerful friends to her lost husband, and to her noble house; she hoped that nothing was necessary for her deliverance, and for the punishment of her oppressors, but to inform them of her dangerous and distressful state. Possessed with these thoughts, she conceived the bold design, of eluding the vigilance of Raymond, and of escaping to a religious house: there to take sanctuary with her infant son, from thence to represent to the King, the cruel insult offered to the memory of his kinsman and faithful soldier, and to demand redress of his and her own wrongs from the justice of the throne, and the power of her friends. She took no pains to conceal these sentiments; but freely communicated the design to Elinor, and entreated her assistance. She enlarged on the power and opportunities of rewarding her fidelity, which success must give her: she lavishly poured out gold and jewels. "Go," said she, "find among the dependants of this proud Lord, if there be courage and humanity in any breast to favour a virtuous design. Here are rewards! a small portion and but an earnest of that munificence with which my gratitude shall repay the benefit." The attendant at first seemed astonished at the boldness of the attempt: whilst the Countess renewed her solicitations, a new and sudden thought seemed to start to life within her mind: but before she could give it utterance, their conversation was interrupted; and Elinor commanded to attend instantly on Lord Raymond. She departed with a look, which assured the Countess of her unalterable attachment; but did not entirely dissipate her terrors. These were instantly awakened at the alarm of every thing new and unexpected.

A long interval of suspense increased her anxiety: at length however the faithful attendant returned, and with a cheerful aspect. "Dearest Lady," said she, "the blessed saints seem to encourage us to the bold attempt of escaping from these walls. Lord Raymond hath appointed his Knights to make ready in three days to accompany him to the neighbouring woods; there, to pursue the chase. He hath enquired of your health: and is persuaded that you continue ill at ease. He hath enjoined the exactest care and vigilance in his absence, and particularly that none be suffered to approach your chamber, but in my presence and by my appointment. The command of the castle is to be committed to my brother: and strict ward to be maintained. But he is no friend to oppression. I have already sounded, and find him apt to our purpose." Ela passionately entreated that this man should be brought before her: but soon recollecting the necessity of avoiding all suspicion, she contented herself with entrusting to Elinor the important charge of prevailing on him. Into her hands she earnestly gave up all her store of wealth: and the good attendant prudently and faithfully employed such part of it as was necessary to confirm the wavering resolution of her brother. She prevailed, and returned with the pleasing tidings that he had consented to follow the fortunes of the Countess, and to seize the approaching occasion to convey her and her young son to any place of safety. In the meantime she advised that Ela should still continue the appearance of malady and weakness, and patiently wait the happy moment of her deliverance. The eyes of this lady brightened up with joy and pleasure, and her breast laboured with the violent emotions of gratitude. "Gracious powers!" (thus her passions forced their way) "Is this the vassal of an unjust oppressor? This the agent of tyranny and cruelty? Say, whence hath thy gentle manners been so strangely associated with savage pride, and usurpation? Whence hath thy goodness and affection been chosen by Lord Raymond to minister to his purposes? Who art thou, that feelest my affliction, and art thus kindly solicitous for my relief?" The attendant wept, and thus returned answer to the enquiries of the Countess.

SECTION III

"Happier days have I beheld; and better fortune have I experienced. I had a husband, lady, brave and honest: a son too, trained to arms, and exercised in deeds of war.—But heaven was pleased to take them from me."—Here her grief broke forth with still greater violence, and redoubled the attention of the Countess; nor did she soon recover such ease as enabled her to proceed in the following manner.

"Our residence was in the neighbourhood of Nottingham, where we lived in peace, removed from the cares of greatness, and the bitterness of distress. My husband was loving; Edmund our only child, the delight of our eyes, and comfort of our advancing years. Though bred to arms, he was mild and gentle, and though nurtured in the humble vale of life, he was brave and generous. Even from his infant years, he had conceived an affection for the daughter (she too the only child) of a neighbouring Franklin, which grew with their ripening age; nor was condemned or controlled. The fond parents beheld this youthful pair of lovers with secret joy; and hoped, in them, to transmit their names and little inheritances to succeeding times. They were betrothed, and but waited for the holy benediction to crown their wishes; when war and tumult began to rage in England. John was then our King: he had submitted, and was reconciled to the Holy Father. He had attempted to recover his dominions in France; but, abandoned by his discontented Nobles, he returned to his kingdom, full of vexation and revenge. Ah, Lady! little doth the high-born Courtier or the powerful Lord conceive of that weight of misery which public dissensions heap upon the lowly subject! The King marched like an enemy through the land, spoiling and ravaging the estates of his wayward Barons. He arrived at Nottingham; where my Lord of Canterbury, at length, prevailed to stop his unfriendly progress. He continued here for some time: his followers, secure in his protection, and enriched by his bounty, little regarded the severe limits which laws prescribe. Gay revellers they; who, full of mirth and disport, beguiled the time in song and dance with courtly dames. One of these glittering minions of royal favour perchance cast his wanton eyes on Edyth, the maid betrothed to my son. Accursed be the hour, in which he discovered, and was enamoured with her beauty! He courted her in gentle guise, with fair semblance of respect and decent love:

he dazzled her with the view of costly gifts; he promised much, he sighed often, and sometimes wept; but all-fruitless were his endeavours to conquer the integrity of this honest maiden. Yet, not entirely displeased at his flattering arts, she listened without terror or abhorrence, whilst yet his purpose was not directly avowed; and sometimes, yielding to his courtesy, suffered him to lead her forth, and to amuse her ear with tales of courtly pleasures and splendour. The jealous anxiety of Edmund ever watched their steps at wary distance: 'till at length, when this incautious maid had been conducted to a secret path, when she suddenly found her helpless innocence at the mercy of a luxurious courtier; when he boldly pressed his suit, and attempted to force her, trembling and dismayed, to his wicked purpose, her piercing shrieks soon summoned a faithful deliverer to her side. Edmund, mad with rage and jealousy, fatally smote the ravisher; and carelessly leaving him weltering in blood, conveyed away his Edyth, who had fainted with terror and surprise, and safely deposited his heart's dear treasure in her father's dwelling.

"An event like this was not to be concealed: nor did the unhappy youth, now mad with passion, and deaf to the calls of prudence, fear to avow his bloody deed freely and publicly. Soon was the body discovered; and soon was Edmund seized, and torn from his frantic mistress. An armed band hurried him away, with loud and tumultuous denunciations of vengeance; when happily the King, now returning from the chase, descried the rout, and dispatched an attendant to demand the cause of such disorder. Of this he was instantly informed; and curious to learn the occasion of such a presumptuous violence upon his officer, to view the man who even boasted of his outrage, he ordered the criminal to be brought before him. My son was now led forward; and as he prepared to cast himself at the feet of his Liege, the fiery beast which the King bestrode, frighted at the tumult, began to start and rear up with ungovernable wildness. The attendants instantly alighted; but before they could support their falling master, Edmund had burst like lightning from the hands of his guards, broke his fall, and remounted him. This zeal and vigour were beheld with wonder, and secret applause. The King himself was by no means unaffected by the incident. His looks grew less severe; and in a tone, not angry, but majestically grave, he demanded to know who he was, and what had prompted him to this act of blood. My son kneeled before him, modest but not abject; and with an ingenuous plainness and freedom, related the unhappy cause that had provoked him to this outrage: his love to the betrothed maid; the arts and treachery to which she had been exposed; the horrid attempt of violation; and his own fatal encounter with the King's officer. In a word, he acknowledged the crime, and with decent boldness declared himself resigned to the punishment, and prepared to yield up his forfeit life. The King listened with attention, and in the natural and unaffected narrative saw the full proof of all that had been alleged. With a sudden warmth, he swore by the foot of God, (his usual oath) that his servant had deservedly met his fate; that Edmund was a brave youth, and merited not only pardon, but reward; and that henceforward he should be his soldier. The witnesses of this scene were not slow to applaud the sentiments of their sovereign. They vied with each other in their praises of my son, whose youthful breast was but too susceptible of their impressions. How happy did we then esteem ourselves, when we saw our child rescued from destruction, graced with the royal favour, and entrusted with an honourable command! To us he paid his filial duty; then flew to the beloved Edyth, to comfort her sorrow and revive her spirit, confounded and depressed by the late event. Of her, he took a tender leave, with assurances of invariable fidelity, and passionate vows of speedy return to complete his happiness; then departed to perform the duties of his new charge. But we were not as yet totally bereft of our darling object; some intervals he found for brief, yet frequent visitings; to delight us with the accounts of his advancing fortune. So completely was he now possessed with the thoughts of war and honour; so elevated and transported by the view of courtly splendour, and the gay promises of youthful ambition, that love seemed to hold but a second place within his mind: and the sighs and half-suppressed tears of Edyth, sometimes confessed her jealous fear of his estrangement. He saw, and chid her unjust suspicions: to allay them, he proposed that the holy father should instantly unite their hands. Their nuptials were sudden; and their conjugal endearments, alas! too soon interrupted by our son's necessary attendance on his royal master.

"The land was now threatened with all the calamities of civil war. A second time had the bold Barons put on their armour, and collected their vassals against John. My husband, although he had already suffered in their cause, yet still adhered with an obstinate integrity to that side which he deemed the great bulwark of his country. He earnestly pressed young Edmund to abandon the service of a prince whose favour was precarious; suddenly and capriciously bestowed; and as suddenly and capriciously withdrawn. But he was heard with reluctance and aversion. He urged the solid comforts of honest poverty and contentment; he called it shameful (forgive me, Lady, if his homely sentiments offend) to unite with rapacious foreigners, and to imbrue his hands in the blood of countrymen and brethren. His son was still unmoved, and to all his arguments opposed one plea, his forfeit life, and the vast debt of gratitude he owed the King. A father's authority was then exerted. He was commanded, upon his filial obedience, to attend on the confederated lords; the terrors of divine vengeance were denounced on his undutiful obstinacy. He hesitated; but the flattering prospects of ambition at length prevailed. He forgot the submission due to a parent's authority; full of gay hopes and impatient of control, he hastened away to serve his liege lord, whilst my husband, irritated at his disobedience, pronounced something like a curse upon his unhappy son, and followed the standard of William de Albinet the commanding Baron.

"Through the course of these unhappy contests, Edmund increased in honour; and still more and more approved his active valour. It is too well known with what shameful disregard to the protection of their adherents, the Barons suffered a number of the most faithful to their cause to be shut up within the castle of Rochester, and to be sorely pressed by the royal army, while they themselves rioted in London. In a fatal hour, Edmund was commanded to the siege of this castle.—O Lady! a few words are sufficient for the rest of his sad story. How doth the dreadful remembrance pierce my afflicted heart! Many deeds of manhood did he achieve; and oftentimes did he repel the desperate valour of the besieged. At the head of a small party, he at length ventured too rashly to approach the castle walls; and was suddenly encountered by a larger body of the enemy. The contest was obstinate and bloody: but his associates were borne down by numbers, and left him, as they yielded, singly engaged with a soldier, whose sword threatened destruction. They rushed upon each other, they closed, they redoubled their deadly blows, 'till at length, a well directed stroke from the arm of Edmund fell upon the front of his antagonist, cleft his beaver, and uncovered his wounded head. Edmund started! stood aghast! uttered some confused sounds of horror! How can I speak it!—The ill-fated youth—O forever accursed be the authors of every civil strife!—had smote his father."—Here the disorder of the unhappy mother stopped her voice. The Countess was scarcely less affected: she trembled, as if witness of the horrid scene: and Elinor at length proceeded thus.

"My husband, stunned and faint, was sinking down; when Edmund seized him in his arms, and gently laid him upon the earth. He kneeled before him, in all the bitterness of anguish and distraction. His lamentations were loud and wild; and earnestly did he implore for pardon; and bitterly did he curse his own fatal error. The languid eyes of his father were fixed kindly upon him; his faltering voice spoke forgiveness. And now was Edmund preparing to bind up his wound, and to convey him to some place of safety and relief, when the noise of tumult and rout grew loud. He turned his head hastily, to learn the cause; and, in that fatal moment, received a shot from a crossbow full in his brain. The son sunk down by the side of the bleeding father; the routed, and the pursuers (a party of the royal army who had come to the support of their associates) trampled upon their bodies. Edmund had at once expired with a groan. My husband lived but to relate the dreadful story."

Here the attendant struggled to suppress her sorrow. Not so the gentle Countess. Her tender mind was deeply pierced; and freely was her pity uttered.—"Thus," said Elinor, "in one accursed hour, was I bereft of all my comfort. The calamity was too great for my weak heart to bear. The relation instantly confused my brain, and deprived me of reason. Long did I continue in a melancholy insensibility to my distress; and perhaps, heaven was kind in thus afflicting me. When time, and a brother's tender care, had at length restored my disordered senses, I learned, that the wretched Edyth had been seized with the pangs of untimely childbirth, had with pain and sorrow given her lifeless burden to the light, long languished in sickness and grief; and was at length retired to a religious house, there to end her wretched days. And there were they soon ended. I myself had been despoiled of all my possessions, by the fury of civil war, in which both parties were equally incensed against my husband or my son. Rescued from death, and supported by the kindness of my brother, the vassal of Lord Raymond; him have I followed, and by his means have I been placed here; ready to obey our Lord in all humble and honest duties: but we have not yet learned to be the base instruments of oppression."—Here she paused and wept. The Countess laboured to comfort, and to inspire her with hopes of better fortune; repeated her assurances of favour and protection; and earnestly declared, that to be happy, she had but to extricate a grateful mistress from her present distress.

SECTION IV

The long wished for day at length appeared, when Raymond and his Knights were to issue forth, and Oswald the brother of Elinor was to be warder of the castle. The time and manner of escape had been duly concerted. The garb of an humble domestic had been provided for the Countess: in which disguise, she, together with her son and faithful woman, were to be conveyed through a postern gate, which led to a neighbouring wood: there was Oswald to provide horses, and from thence to conduct them to a religious house, which had been enriched by the pious bounty of Ela, in her more prosperous days: and where she now hoped to find due regard, and inviolable sanctuary. The day was spent in preparation; in fears and hopes, and anxiety. At length the mid-hour of night approached, the hour appointed for departure. Oswald by means of a trusty servant had placed his horses in the wood; and had so stationed his men as to prevent them from being witnesses of his design. The Countess had put on her disguise, embraced her son, and delivered him to the hand of Elinor. Their conductor led them cautiously and silently through the castle. They had passed the gate, and were now stretching towards the wood with more enlivened steps, when the shrill sound of a horn proceeded from the other side of the castle, and proclaimed the approach of some knight or stranger. Oswald started, the women trembled; the sound was loudly repeated, and returned from the adjacent hills. When Oswald, marking where the full moon disclosed a beaten path, and pointing towards the wood, earnestly pressed them to bend their course thither without fear or hesitation, and there to wait his coming; which he promised should be speedy. He spoke of the present alarm as of no moment, but declared himself resolved to learn the occasion of it. They obeyed; and he returned into the castle: where he appeared opportunely to prevent suspicion or detection. The domestics were all roused, and some had already mounted the battlements to demand, who, at this dead hour, had approached the castle, and on what occasion. They were answered, that there stood two persons at the gates dispatched by Hubert chief justiciary, to Lord Raymond on especial affairs; that they had been misguided, and wandered through the country until night had overtaken them: that at length they had recovered the true path, and that their fatigue required immediate entrance and refreshment. By the command of Oswald, they were admitted and entertained with due courtesy. He, though determined to abandon the service of Raymond, and impatient to rejoin the Countess and her son, yet could not resist the desire of conferring with these messengers; and especially when he learned from one of them, who seemed of inferior quality, that they brought some intelligence about Lord Salisbury. He invited this man to refresh himself with wine (for the other had retired to rest.) He entertained him with all hospitable kindness, and from him learned, that but a little time since, solemn jousts and tournaments had been held at the English court, in which a young knight of France (induced, as he declared, by the fame of the gallant Nobles of Britain) had appeared, and distinguished himself by his prowess and courage. That the King and his courtiers had received him with all due honours: that in some conversations, he had lamented the fate of an English Lord known in both realms by the name of Salisbury: who, as he was informed, had been pursued by adverse fortune in Poictieu, obliged to fly before his enemies, abandoned by his few attendants, and accompanied only by a fair and noble lady; and that too strong reasons there were to fear that he had perished. Oswald heard him with a violent yet well-dissembled emotion; and having prevailed on him to retire, paused, though still anxious to seek the Countess, and debated within his mind, whether he should communicate this intelligence or no. As he was not sufficiently acquainted with the refined and exalted sentiments of noble minds, he concluded that the hopes of her Lord's return were Ela's only motive for receiving the addresses of Lord Raymond with such severity and abhorrence, and that any assurances of his death must determine her to accept the tenders of his love: he therefore resolved freely to declare what he had just now heard; and hoped that she might thus be prevailed on to abandon the design of flying, and to return to her castle.

The domestics were now separated; and silence and tranquillity again restored: when Oswald again issued forth, still firmly resolved to obey the commands of the Countess, whatever these might be, and faithfully to follow her fortunes, should she be still resolute to tempt the dangers of flight. He found her at the appointed station impatient of his tedious absence, and almost sinking under the terrors of night and solitude. Elinor sat by her side, still more dismayed, supporting her young son, and shielding him from the dampy air whilst he lay composed in peaceful sleep. The moon was hastening to her decline; and threatened to involve them in all the horrors of darkness; when their long expected protector at length appeared to relieve their distracting fears. He briefly related the occasion of his delay; the arrival of these messengers, and the discourse which he had held with one of them. The bare mention of intelligence about Lord William, raised an universal agitation in the Countess. The melancholy air which Oswald assumed, increased her terror and impatience: nor had he yet finished his relation, when the blood deserted the cheeks of Ela. She closed her eyes, and died away. Elinor shrieked, Oswald supported her; but their cares were a long time ineffectual. At length, the Countess raised her languid front, and breathed a heart-felt sigh. "He was then disloyal!" said she:—"A noble lady!—was she noble?—But alas, I fear, heaven hath severely punished his guilt." Oswald now perceived his own imprudence, and would have offered comfort: but the Countess was wholly engaged by her own sad thoughts. He repeatedly pressed and enforced the danger of her present situation, and the necessity of speedy departure: but no attention could he gain. At length, turning her sadly streaming eyes slowly upon him; "No, my friend!" said she, "these languid limbs must here find their grave.—Yet—it were a blessing to end my days in the mansions of devotion, to hear the reverend father speak comfort to my departing spirit:—but, I cannot—this frame is too feeble: the hand of death presses too severely upon me—O friends! if ever your hearts knew pity, look upon that boy. He was not born to this wretchedness: he hath still noble friends.—If you would atone to heaven for your offences, save him; convey him quickly from the power of his enemies. Seek the place appointed for our retreat; there save yourselves and him: there shall the friends of his house find him rescued from cruelty and usurpation: they shall protect and defend him; they shall assert his rights and reward your fidelity. These jewels, these treasures shall reward you. My son shall live to reward you."—Elinor, kneeling before her with weeping eyes and lifted hands, earnestly entreated her to collect her spirits and to pursue her intended flight: uttering the most ardent and passionate vows that fear or force should never drive her from her beloved mistress.—"If I am beloved," said the Countess, "show me thy love; and save my child. Think not of me. I can die here: and some charitable hand may perhaps be found to close my eyes in peace." Here she again fainted; nor could all the tender care and solicitude exerted to relieve her, restore her to life and sense. Elinor hung weeping over her: Oswald was dismayed and distracted: he saw the danger of this rash enterprise, and could think of no resource: he would have consulted with his sister; but her mind was engaged only by her mistress. He suddenly called to his attendant, who still continued at some distance with the horses: one of these he mounted: the Countess was raised up and placed reclining in his arms. Thus he proceeded gently towards a cottage which lay at some small distance; whose charitable inhabitants rose at the noise of benighted travellers, and admitted them. The Countess was disposed upon their humble couch, and now once again recovered from her trance. She thanked the tenderness of the afflicted Elinor: then calling to Oswald, with hands and eyes raised to heaven, she earnestly conjured him by all his hopes of future happiness, to fly with her son to sanctuary: to proclaim his and her wrongs: and particularly to seek the protection of the Lord de Warren his father's noble friend; who would receive and shield his helpless innocence, assert his rights, and control his oppressors. Of herself she spake with indifference; as a person on the point of finding refuge from her enemies in the arms of death. Oswald was so persuaded: he regarded her present languid state as the last sad period of her life; and looking tenderly upon his sister, seemed to wish that she could fly from the resentment of Lord Raymond. But soon were his thoughts checked by the zealous declarations of this friendly matron, that no fear of power, no threats of punishment, no motive whatever should prevail upon her to abandon her dear mistress: she urged him to obey her commands with speed, and to leave them to the protection of heaven. The honest heart of Oswald was affected: in a passionate fit of zeal, he declared himself ready to fly with young William. The anxious mother thanked him with her looks: she clasped her son with a feeble but tender embrace; and lifting her eyes devoutly towards heaven, commended him to the protection of all the holy angels. His looks confessed his infant fear, when she delivered him to his conductor. He wept, and was conveyed away. Some few tears dropped from the Countess; but the recollection of his escape, and the hopes of his preservation, soon gave comfort to her afflicted mind, and animated her with new life and spirit. Her eyes were lighted up anew; her voice less faltering, and her frame less languid. She now seemed to defy her oppressors, and declared herself resolved to assume her rightful authority and state; to act as mistress of her castle and domain, in open defiance of the bold intruders. By the dawn of morning, some peasants were dispatched to the castle to give notice of her present situation, and to order such conveniences as were necessary for her removal. A litter together with the proper attendants was soon sent for this purpose. Elinor, still faithful to her charge, waited on the side of her beloved lady: who now again entered her own stately hall, and was laid with care and tender offices of duty upon her own couch.

SECTION V

In the meantime, confusion had spread among the domestics. Morning discovered the desertion of Oswald; and scarcely had messengers been dispatched to inform Lord Raymond of this event, and the arrival of the two strangers, when they learned the situation of the Countess, and were directed to conduct her back to her apartment. A second message was instantly dispatched to their Lord, with this alarming intelligence: and, ere long, he appeared in view, goring the sides of his courser, whilst a few attendants stretched after him at some distance, in vain striving to keep pace with his impatience. He entered the castle with looks wild and disordered; and flew towards the apartment of the Countess; but was stopped by some of her maidens, who were directed to inform him that her present weakness and malady required rest, and could not permit him to approach. He called for Elinor, who appeared before him trembling. He sternly reproached her with presumptuous treachery and disobedience; and demanded to know where her brother lay concealed, whither and for what purpose he had fled. Elinor still trembled and was silent: Raymond thundered out terrible denunciations of vengeance; when the Countess, who heard his rage from the adjacent chamber, suddenly sent to desire his presence. He rushed in with glaring looks of fury and distraction; when, rising her head gently from her pillow, Ela thus accosted him. "Proud Lord, thy power is at an end. I am above thy oppression; I am hastening to the mansions of peace. My son is safe. Yes! that honest man has conveyed him to the neighbouring monastery, whose hallowed sanctuary shall protect him from thee and thy minions. Thither thou canst not force thy way. Thence, shall our wrongs be boldly and loudly echoed through the land, and soon shall the noble friends of Salisbury appear, to end thy usurpation, to challenge thy ministers of cruelty, and to revenge the injuries done even to the meanest of Ela's attendants."—Thus speaking, she turned away with marks of scorn; again reclined her head, nor deigned the least regard to his extravagant expressions of vexation and surprise. He burst away in mad disorder and confusion: he ranged wildly through the galleries; started, and endeavoured to collect his thoughts and allay his passions: cursed his own rash folly which had attempted him abroad, afforded this opportunity of detecting and defeating his designs, and threatened to cover him with shame and scorn. Then again he rushed forward in an agony of rage and vexation, when one of the messengers from Hubert approached with respectful obeisance; and obliged him to assume some appearance of ease and composure.

From him Lord Raymond learned the several particulars, which his companion had before imparted to Oswald. But as this man was admitted more intimately into the confidence of Hubert, he was farther directed to declare, that the friends to the house of Salisbury began to express their fears, that the long protracted residence of Raymond in this castle, without any intelligence being received of the dispositions of the Countess, any assurances of her consent to accept his hand, had raised jealousies and sus-picions in their minds; and that Hubert therefore urged him to renew his efforts, if he still continued unsuccessful; to improve those rumours about Earl William, into full and certain assurances of his death, and with all possible speed and earnestness to hasten on his own nuptials with the Countess. He thanked the stranger, and commended his fidelity; he requested him to retire for a while, prom-ising to confer more fully with him at better leisure: then resigned himself to the disorder of his mind, which this information and advice served to inflame and irritate. He now saw the misguided course which he had pursued. He formed the most dreadful presages of that dishonour which must attend his violence and unlawful oppression. His passion for the Countess was still alive; and for a while he seemed resolved once more to try the gentle arts of love and tenderness; but the recollection of her rigour and disdain, her wrongs and sufferings, in a moment dashed all his hopes, and he resolved to fall at her feet, to implore her pardon, and to retire from her castle. For this purpose he again approached her apartment, and demanded ad-mittance. Elinor appeared before him, kneeled, and with many tears implored his indulgence for the weak state of her unhappy Lady. "Heaven only knows," said the kind attendant, "whether she hath yet a few days of life remain-ing. Let not thy noble nature afflict the already too severely afflicted. Let her die in peace; or if she may yet live, break not on that tranquillity which may be the happy means of restoring her." "Wretch!" cried Raymond, wildly surveying her, as she humbled herself before him, "thou hast undone me! Accursed be the slave who hath assisted thee to betray me! But why do I think of thee, thou reptile? Come, lead me to this Lady; let me dispel her maladies, let me give her peace, and leave her."—Elinor started up, confounded and astonished at this mysterious language, earnest for an explanation, yet too much awed and terrified to speak her wishes. Raymond sternly repeated his orders; and in that moment, the inhuman Grey, with all marks of haste and impatience, rushed impetuously into the apartment.

He had heard of the escape and return of the Countess, and of the flight of Oswald. He had spurred on with wild speed to learn more particularly the reason and purpose of these alarming events; his own conscious guilt had raised dreadful presages in his mind: nor were these allayed by the disorder in which he now found Lord Raymond. To him he addressed some hasty and imperfect questions. Raymond gazed on him for a while with an aspect which plainly discovered an inward strife, and doubt whether to accuse this man as his evil counsellor, or to entreat his assistance as a faithful friend. At length, as if bowed down by violence of passion, he reclined on his arm, and was led away into another apartment. There he distinctly recounted the advices he had received from Hubert; and the jealousies expressed by the friends of the house of Salisbury, which must now be inflamed and confirmed by the false Oswald, who had fled to sanctuary with young William. He spoke with pity and tenderness of the Countess, whom his own cruelty had driven from her castle, and whose flight had been prevented only by her malady and weakness. He expressed his fears of detection and dishonour; that his unwarrantable usurpation, and attempt upon the constancy of Ela, must now cover him with shame: he therefore declared himself resolved to implore her forgiveness, and to retire. The coward heart of Grey felt all the terrors that Raymond had expressed with double force. He was instantly filled with the imagination of that power and protection which were soon to support the injured Countess: he trembled at the recollection of his own share of guilt and oppression: he commended the purpose of Lord Raymond; and urged him to resign his pretensions without delay. But amidst all his fears, cunning had not yet forsaken him. He secretly determined to make this resolution of his Lord seem the effect of his own advice, in order to plead some merit with the Countess, and, in some measure, to atone for his former insolence. He therefore proposed to Raymond, to make him the messenger of his design, to entrust him with the charge of acquainting Ela with his penitence, and his resignation of all hopes or pretensions to her love or fortune. "An interview," said he, "can only serve to inflame your fond passion, and to make a separation doubly painful. No! trust not your eyes with the too powerful and affecting object." Raymond consented; and Grey now prepared to summon Elinor, and to desire admission to the Countess; when accidentally, he asked Lord Raymond, who still dwelt upon the late events, to what place of sanctuary Oswald had retired. The neighbouring monastery of Sarum was no sooner mentioned, than, suddenly starting, as if a ray of comfort had just shot through his soul, his eyes kindled, his cheeks glowed, his whole aspect spoke surprise and triumph: he eagerly seized the hand of his astonished Lord; he paused; their eyes encountered each other. "Hope!" said Grey; "yet hope!—I must depart this instant.—But, by all your fond wishes, by all your flattering prospects of love and greatness, I conjure you suspend your purpose: see not, speak not to this proud Countess, 'till my return." Raymond demanded an explanation, but Grey only repeated his injunctions; urged him to retire, and left him filled with astonishment and expectation.

Book IV

SECTION I

In the religious house to which Oswald had retired, was a Monk, called Reginhald, whose mind but ill-suited his profession, or his residence in a seat of piety. He was brother to Grey, and by his interest had been not long since admitted into the monastery, and promoted to some degree of dignity and authority. His manners were equally brutal with those of Grey, but less disguised by art and hypocrisy. He was, like him, abject and servile, but by no means so well skilled in the arts of flattery: insolent and assuming, but not careful to distinguish between those who feared and those who defied his power. Hence was he frequently controlled and mortified by his brethren, whom he dreaded from a consciousness of his own excesses; and who detested and scorned him indeed, yet feared the power which supported, or seemed to support him. They regarded his brother as the favourite of Lord Raymond, and Lord Raymond as heir to the house of Salisbury, and already possessed of all its greatness. To purchase his protection, therefore, they turned their eyes from his offences, and suffered him to disgrace and disturb their house by scandalous excesses, utterly subversive of holy discipline and order. Drunkenness, and riot, and lewdness, had oftentimes profaned their walls with impunity. They lamented these enormities of their unworthy brother; but, instead of disclosing and punishing them, lamented to each other in secret, lest they should forfeit the favour and protection of Lord Raymond; although the miscreant had been scarcely known, and was utterly unnoticed and disregarded by this Lord.

Grey had conceived a sudden hope of preventing the effects which the flight of Oswald threatened, by means of this Reginhald; and, if not of gaining young William into his own power, at least of preventing any emissaries from spreading the intelligence of his escape to sanctuary, and the distresses of his mother. That it was that determined him to depart instantly, and to visit this monastery: but his brother, active and officious in every deed of baseness, had already prevented his desires. Oswald had happily reached the monastery, and Reginhald was among the first to demand the reason of his appearance. Scarcely could he restrain his passion until Oswald had completed his story; and, then, burst forth with unbounded rage into the vilest and severest reproaches. He charged him with falsehood and treachery; declared himself resolved instantly to learn the real nature of his crime, and purpose of his flight; and, for this reason, to repair in person to the castle. In the meantime, with an assumed air of authority he ordered that this fugitive should be strictly guarded, and kept from all intercourse till his return. Oswald heard his brutal virulence and passion, not without some terror, which was noted, and regarded as an indication of guilt. The directions of Reginhald were obeyed, and he himself now hastened to inform his brother of this event. He met him when he had but just rode a few paces from the castle; whither Grey instantly returned with the Monk.

They retired to a private conference with equal eagerness, and with minds equally prepared for outrage or treachery. The Monk prevented the enquiries of his brother, by relating what had just now passed at the monastery. Grey expressed a sullen joy, when informed that Oswald was closely guarded, and, for the present, effectually prevented from spreading his saucy tale, or pursuing the design for which he had fled. He commended the zeal of Reginhald; and, seizing his arm with an aspect, earnest, and mysteriously solemn, he declared, that both their future fortunes depended on confining Oswald from all intercourse and gaining young William into their own power and disposal. The rude Monk, whose first thoughts were ever to recur to violence, instantly declared for seizing both, and forcing them from their retreat: but he was stopped by Grey, who censured such procedure as dangerous and unwarrantable; and pronounced it necessary to pursue measures the most deliberate and most cautiously concerted. He proceeded to disclose all the transactions of Lord Raymond from his first arrival at the castle of Salisbury, all the efforts made to shake the constancy of Ela, and all the opposition and disdain of that proud Countess. He began to explain how much their fortunes must be advanced by finding means of conquering her resolution, and by the final success of Lord Raymond in obtaining full and indisputable possession of the lands and dignities of the house of Salisbury. But Reginhald, conscious that his own security from disgrace and punishment depended on the influence and protection of this Lord, needed no inducement to concur in the designs and practices of his brother. He broke in upon his discourse with a passionate heat, and loudly condemned all his late proceedings. "Why," said he, "was not I made acquainted with your difficulties? why were not their hands forcibly joined? I should have at once pronounced the nuptial benediction over them, and, without regard to female pride or scruples, have united them forever in those bands, which no human power can rend asunder."—Grey again began to condemn his violence, and to urge the necessity of caution, when their conference was suddenly interrupted by a domestic, who surprised them by declaring that he sought the Monk, and had in charge to conduct him to the Countess.

The mind of this unhappy Lady had long been violently agitated, the true cause of that languor and malady which oppressed her gentle frame. The hopes she had conceived of the safety of her son, and the speedy arrival of friends and deliverers, had acted on her harassed spirits like a powerful medicine, and checked the progress of her disorder. She had now leisure to turn her thoughts to her husband, and to weigh those accounts of his fate which Oswald had rashly conveyed to her. The idea of his disloyalty was piercing: she revolved it frequently; she reasoned on the intelligence she had received; she believed; she doubted; she indulged her suspicions; and strove to banish them, by turns. Ill were those reflections suited to restore her impaired health; yet she dwelt upon them. The faithful Elinor, from whom she could not conceal her thoughts, in vain endeavoured to compose her distractions, and to allay her inward grief: still she tormented herself with reflections on the supposed falsehood of her Lord, and on his unhappy fate; when the attendant casually discovered from a window the approach of Reginhald, and observed with some surprise that a religious man, who by his habit seemed of the neighbouring monastery, was now entering the castle. "He comes with news of my son," said the Countess hastily; "Let him be called hither.—And, alas, this distracted breast hath but too much need of spiritual counsel and comfort."

A domestic was instantly dispatched to seek the Monk; who now appeared before the Countess. Naturally base and mean, and never before admitted into such a presence, he stood abashed and confused; and the consciousness of his own vile purposes served to increase his disorder. His aspect, in which the sensual and malignant passions had fixed their seat, and his deportment, which was that of the rude hind or midnight brawler, not of the holy and lettered clerk, were surveyed by the Countess with sudden disgust. She shuddered, as at the view of some loathsome animal: yet, assuming a placid air, and endeavouring to conceal her dislike, she asked of his order and residence. No sooner had he named the brotherhood of Sarum, than raising herself from the couch on which she leaned, "You then," said she, "bring me news of my son—dispatched to acquaint me with his safe arrival within your holy walls— Is it not so?" Reginhald coldly answered, that her son was safe, and had been deposited in the monastery by his conductor. The Countess, with clasped hands and earnest accents, uttered a prayer for his protection. Elinor was tenderly affected; and, uniting her fervours with those of her beloved mistress, commended young William to every saint and holy angel. The Monk stood unmoved, and scarcely could assume the appearance of devotion, just so far as to pronounce a cold assent to their petitions. The Countess was on the point of imploring his protection for her son, but the disgust which she had conceived at his aspect, and which was increased by his demeanour, re-pressed that thought. She contented herself with speaking her hopes in general, that his innocence and his wrongs would not fail to raise him friends in the house of piety and charity. She spoke of the oppression which she herself had suffered, in terms of bitterness and indignation: and seemed to demand, as her just right, the vigorous interpo-sition of every good man for her relief, but more especially the dutiful and faithful offices of those holy men who had experienced her favour and munificence. The silence of

Reginhald gave her an occasion of repeating and enforcing her discourse: but her discourse was directed to an unfriendly ear. The wicked Monk had fixed his eyes upon an object, which totally diverted his attention from the Countess. Near her couch there stood a table, on which, among some female ornaments, was deposited a ring, an ancient and precious jewel, which had long been the distinguishing ornament of her noble house, and bore its ensigns armorial curiously impressed. The sight of this instantly suggested a treacherous purpose to the Monk; for which it was necessary to possess himself of the jewel. His situation was convenient for seizing it, unnoticed by Ela or her attendant. He watched a favourable moment to convey it to his bosom; and, having once secured his prize, he was more at leisure to answer the discourse of the Countess, to assume some appearance of gravity, and to affect the dignity and spiritual authority of his function. He declared, that, within their walls, her son could not suffer wrong: but that it was unnecessary to send him thither for protection. Nature and the royal pleasure pointed to his noble kinsman Raymond as his true protector.—The Countess prepared to express her indignation, but with an insolence which he mistook for grave authority; he warned her to beware of froward pride. "Their liege Lord," he said, "had graciously considered her widowed state, and provided relief and comfort.—Her hand, her affection, and her obedience were now due to Lord Raymond: such was the King's command. Heaven had approved his kind purpose, and would not fail to punish that obstinacy and haughty perverseness, which rejected its blessings."—"And darest thou, abandoned and hateful wretch,"—thus did the Countess suffer her virtuous anger to break forth: "Darest thou profane the name of heaven? art thou devoted to its service, and dost thou flatter the baseness, and wouldst thou promote the lewd purposes of him who hath renounced its laws, and defies its vengeance?"—"Thy obstinacy be upon thine own head!" This was the reply of Reginhald, who was hardened against all reproof, and impatient to seek his brother. He turned away in sullen disdain, and left the Countess in wonder and just resentment at his brutal insolence; nor did this interview tend to allay the fears and suspicions of a fond mother. "If the oppression of Lord Raymond could have its ministers and favourers among the professed votaries of religion, where might innocence find refuge; or where seek its just redress?" She now dreaded that the sacred privileges of sanctuary might not find the due regard, as her enemy seemed to have corrupted the reverend brethren, and to have gained them over to his wicked purposes. She wished she had contended with her malady, and accompanied her son; again she wished she had not rashly entrusted him to false and treacherous guardians. "Her presence might have proved a sufficient protection to him: Raymond could not dare openly to have raised his arm against him; and surely the outrage and usurpation of this Lord could not long be concealed."—Thus did she condemn her conduct, and torment her soul with gloomy and terrible imaginations; though yet unacquainted with the dangers and distress now prepared for herself and her son.

SECTION II

Reginhald had sought his brother, and recounted all his interview with Ela. Grey still accused him of violence and turbulence, and urged the necessity of well-timed dissimulation, of art, caution, and smooth address. The Monk was provoked at this affectation of superior wisdom; and, instead of retorting his reproof, displayed the stolen jewel, in silent and contemptuous triumph. Grey was too well versed in the arts of fraud and mischief, not to conceive at once, that this ring was to be used for deceiving the brethren of the monastery, or abusing Oswald, as occasions might require, by pretended orders and directions from the Countess. He viewed it eagerly, and regarded it, (not without reason) as an instrument of his purposes, too important to be entrusted wholly to the violent hands of Reginhald. He commended his zeal and address, which, he confidently promised, should, in due time, meet their full reward: he invited him to refreshment; reminded him of his fatigue, and that the hour of rest approached: he promised that, by the dawn of morning, he himself would be ready to accompany him to the monastery, where he made no doubt of happily accomplishing their purposes, and laying a firm foundation of their future fortunes. Reginhald yielded to his instances, and retired. Grey repaired without delay to the apartment of Lord Raymond, and appeared before him with a face of joy and satisfaction. He congratulated him upon the prospect of a speedy and final accomplishment of his wishes: he briefly related the conduct of his brother at the monastery, his reception of Oswald, and the means already taken to prevent that traitor from officiously spreading his tale: he declared his purpose of seeking him instantly in his retirement; and was fully assured, (he said) that, by the assistance of the Monk, (whose zeal and vigilance he praised) he should be able to bring Oswald to that punishment which his falsehood merited, and to gain young William into his absolute disposal, the sure means of prevailing over the pride of Ela, and engaging her to a full compliance with his wishes. Raymond wondered; but Grey repeated his confident assurances of success, and departed with requesting his Lord patiently to wait the events which the succeeding day must produce.

It was now night; but fraud and interested malice are strangers to rest. The Monk was wholly engaged by the thoughts of future favour and preferment; and Grey watched, like the great enemy of mankind, to ensnare the innocent, and to seduce the weak. He busily revolved in his mind the late transactions, and his future designs. He thought of an expedient which Reginhald had mentioned, that of forcibly joining the hands of Raymond and the Countess, and pronouncing the nuptial blessing without regard to her consent; an expedient which he now considered not as the suggestion of rashness and unexperienced heat, but such as the best guided policy might have recourse to, and such as their designs might necessarily require. In the meantime, he resolved, if possible, to reserve the disposal of young William to himself, and even to secrete him from Lord Raymond's power. If this Lord should prove successful, he might forget the services of his creature, or not reward them to the full extent of his wishes. The possession of this boy might hereafter enable him to revenge such neglect, by unexpectedly producing a young heir to assert his rights: or if the Countess should be relieved from her present oppression, and her suitor recalled, or forced from her castle; the important service of restoring her son might atone for his former insolence, and shield him from punishment: or should it be necessary for his purposes to destroy this child; this might be done more securely in some place of private retirement; and more acceptably to his Lord, when executed without his knowledge or participation. His own interest was the sole object of his thoughts; and as to the means of advancing it, to him, all were equally indifferent.

The dawn of morning stole upon him, while he was anxiously engaged in these reflections: and Reginhald now stood before him, urging him to pursue his intended course without further delay. He first summoned some chosen vassals of Raymond, and, in the name of that Lord, ordered them to follow his steps at some distance, and to hold themselves ready to obey his orders. The brothers then took their way, and soon reached the monastery. Here they found that, notwithstanding the directions of Reginhald, the Lord Abbot had been made acquainted with the arrival of Oswald; had examined him in person, had heard, and was duly affected by his story; promised him protection, and that he would assist in all honest means of gaining redress for the injured Countess; and that at this very time he was shut up in the apartment of Oswald, hearing, examining, and enquiring still more minutely into the circumstances of all those events which he related with so much confidence, and with such appearance of integrity. The brothers congratulated each other on arriving so opportunely; and, at their desire, were conducted into the same apartment. Oswald started and trembled at the sight of Grey; who, with a demeanour grave and solemn, and with well affected humility, addressed himself to the Abbot in the following manner:

"Reverend father! This humane attention to the appearance of distress will be rewarded; and heaven forefend but that it should meet the just return of praise from every honest tongue: nor is there less honour due to your pious and charitable cares, because, in the present case, they are not called forth by real danger or calamity. You have entertained a fugitive already pardoned by his Lord; and an infant whom his fond mother is at this moment impatient to embrace.—You wonder: but, vouchsafe me a favourable ear, I shall unfold what seems so strange and perplexing. This venerable brotherhood must have heard, how the royal favour hath been extended to Lord Raymond, hath invested him with all the power and dignity of the house of Salisbury, hath consigned to his protection the widow of that noble house, and destined his hand for that of the gentle Countess. When Raymond first arrived at her castle, to execute the orders of his liege Lord, he found her, alas! sunk deep in sorrowful reflections on the fate of her unhappy Lord, and but ill disposed to listen to his honourable passion; nor could his noble nature permit him to break in too precipitately upon her melancholy, by declaring his suit, and demanding her consent."—Here Oswald would have interrupted his discourse, but Grey, with a mild, yet commanding look, claimed a free and undisturbed audience. The Abbot seemed to assent; and the crafty minion proceeded thus: "A decent interval of retirement was allowed to her grief; and in the meantime her suitor was entertained with the respect due to his greatness: nor was she long a stranger to his purpose; nor did she disdain his suit, although she still deemed it dishonourable openly to admit a second lover, until she had fully paid her duty to the memory of Lord William. In this interval, heaven was pleased to afflict the unhappy Lady with severe sickness: her fever was violent, and long and obstinate was her delirium. She raved, I know not how, of force and oppression; she called upon her late Lord, whom she declared was yet alive, now in her castle, and concealed from her by treachery and cruelty. She spoke of blood, of murder, of her son, his dangers and his enemies. Even when her bodily disorder began to abate, the disorder of her mind was still unconquered: nor were those wild visions yet dispelled, which had so long tormented her. Her discourse indeed seemed more consistent, though the discourse of madness, and, unhappily, imposed on the weakness and inexperience of her attendants. They indulged her madness, and persuaded her to fly, for they believed that Lord Raymond was really her persecutor: who, on his part, was only anxious for her recovery. For this, were his prayers incessantly breathed to heaven. For this, did he bind himself by solemn vow, to reward the devotion of your house, with ample donations: nor was his piety unnoticed, or his prayers rejected. Scarcely had the distraction of this Lady prompted her to send away her son, and to retire from the castle, when heaven was pleased, as it were miraculously, to awaken her from her frightful dreams, and restore her unsettled reason. The first sign of recollection which she discovered, was, her orders to those who had been deceived by her distraction, and rashly conveyed her at midnight from her castle, to conduct her back again. She was obeyed, and instantly called for Lord Raymond, acknowledged her infirmity, and entreated his pardon and indulgence. He, noble and gentle Lord, expressed nothing but the most rapturous joy at this happy change; earnestly pressing her to reward his love, and crown his wishes. No longer now reluctant, or insensible to the happiness which heaven and the royal favour had ordained for her, she only requested that some little respite might still be granted, some time allowed to pay what farther duties the memory of her late Lord demanded. This holy father came opportunely to confirm her in those sentiments, and to direct her pious intentions. By his persuasions am I ordered to attend him hither, directed by Lord Raymond, to enquire by what means and in what manner he may most effectually discharge his vow, and by the gentle Countess to desire, that a solemn requiem shall, without delay, be performed by this reverend brotherhood to her departed Lord. I am still farther to declare, that she reflects with confusion on the late disorder of her mind, which hath driven her young son from her arms; that she is impatient to embrace him; that, at her request to Lord Raymond, he hath freely and fully pardoned the flight of this his attendant. Nothing now remains, but that both return, and share in that general joy which reigns in the castle."—The Abbot wondered, and hesitated; Oswald prepared to speak, but Grey again prevented him.—"To remove doubts, or scruples," said he, turning to Reginhald, "let us produce the token of our truth and fairly-delivered charge. Behold, Lord Abbot, this ancient ring, the well-known signet of the Countess, entrusted to us from her fair hand! By this she speaks her pleasure, that young William be instantly delivered to our care, that, without delay, we may conduct him to her noble presence."

The Abbot had listened with suspicion and distrust, nor was his perplexity dissipated by the conclusion of this speech. The accounts which he had received from Oswald seemed natural and consistent; those of Grey subtle and improbable: and, yet, this ring was such an attestation of his truth and integrity, as seemed to warrant a full assent. He wavered for a while, but endeavoured to persuade himself that the orders which Grey delivered were real, and demanded his compliance; timorous by nature, and possessed with strong imaginations of the power of Raymond, and the danger of his displeasure. He therefore laboured to suppress all his doubts; affected to be fully convinced and satisfied; and consented to deliver up young William to be conducted back to his mother by the Monk and Grey; who dissembled their joy, and studied to complete their success, by seducing Oswald from his retreat. They exerted all their artifice to persuade him that the resentment of his Lord had totally subsided; that he could not but consent to the desires of the gentle Countess, and forgive an honest though mistaken zeal for the service of a Lady, who in a few days was to be united with him, in the bands of love and wedlock. Oswald hesitated; he knew the falsehood of some part of what Grey had declared; yet he conceived that he must have delivered this jewel from the hand of the Countess, and by her command; and that, of consequence, she must have been reconciled to her suitor. He thought it natural, on such a reconciliation, to conceal some late transactions: thus he endeavoured to account for the misrepresentations of Grey: yet still he feared, and doubted.—Grey, as by authority of his Lord, and in his name, not only pronounced his full pardon, but assured him of favour and reward. The Abbot condemned his irresolution as weak and criminal; as highly prejudicial to his own interest, and an undutiful suspicion of the truth and honour of his master. The simplicity and inexperience of the vassal gave force to these solicitations; he dreaded to renew the displeasure of Raymond by delay or hesitation: he consented to return, and resigned himself to Grey, who now led away his victims in triumph.

The party which Grey had appointed to attend him, soon appeared in view, obeyed his signal, and advanced. At the sight of armed men, the misguided Oswald felt all his suspicions renewed; he trembled; and his fears were instantly confirmed. Grey, with an air of sullen authority, ordered him to be seized and bound; he attempted to expostulate, but was silenced with all the insolence of successful malice, committed to a guard, and led away a prisoner to the castle; and, there, was this friend to the afflicted and oppressed consigned to the dreary dungeon. The infant heir of Salisbury was entrusted to others of the party, whose services Grey purchased by rich bribes, and in whom he chiefly confided. A kinsman he had upon the distant coast of Devon, to whom they were directed to convey their charge with strictest care. Thus he resolved to dispose of the young Lord for the present, as he relied on the attachment of this kinsman, and by his means might hereafter remove him to some safe and secret residence, as his future purposes might require.

SECTION III

Thus far the wicked arts of Grey had been completely successful: and, now, he hastened to the presence of Lord Raymond with his flattering congratulations. He acquainted him in a few words, that all the mischief which the flight of Oswald had threatened was now effectually prevented; that he had safely disposed of young William with such guardians as were devoted to his, and to his master's service; and that the false slave who had attempted to betray him, was now his prisoner. Raymond wondered; embraced his minion, and applauded his address and vigilance. In his first violence of pride and resentment he pronounced that Oswald should instantly be hanged upon the next tree. But Grey restrained his passion; and entreated him to suspend the fate of this vassal; and to reserve the power of granting his forfeited life to the requests of Ela, if this might hereafter contribute to conciliate her regards. At the name of Ela, Raymond sighed, and turned upon his creature, with an aspect of perplexity and sorrow. "Trust me," said he, "I am weary of this unprofitable pursuit; and would to heaven I had never seen this proud dame; never felt the power of her beauty!—This morning was I unexpectedly summoned to her presence. I saw the charming mourner: I saw her tortured with fears. She had just discovered the loss of an ancient ring, the usual ornament of her hand, and although she knows not by whom, or for what purpose, it may have been secreted, yet this incident hath awakened her suspicions, and she dreads some farther design upon her peace. But chiefly she fears for her son: she condemns her late conduct as weak and precipitate, and repents of having trusted the boy from her side. At first, she made an effort to preserve her dignity, and, in the language of greatness and affected disdain, demanded how long my usurpation was to be continued. I interrupted her with humble and ardent expressions of love; she wept, and was still deaf to my solicitations. Yet, methought, she spoke of her late Lord with less pride and exultation. 'If,' said she, 'he hath indeed paid the debt of nature, may heaven look on his offences with mercy, and protect his helpless infant, and injured widow!' then, with earnest and affecting accents she entreated me to accept of all her wealth and magnificence, to indulge my wishes freely with the rich inheritance of her lordly house: but not to pursue the ruin of an helpless infant: to suffer his mother to follow him in peace; to hide her grief, and waste her few melancholy days in the holy retirement of the monastery.—O my friend, who could stand unmoved at her disorder? But I did not suffer all my emotion to break out. I contented myself, in general, with entreating her to banish all gloomy thoughts, to expect happy days, to study her real happiness, and to command it. I then retired, impatiently expecting your arrival, and your sage and friendly counsel."

The success which had hitherto attended the practices and designs of Grey, gave him authority and consequence with his Lord, and encouraged him to urge his advice boldly and violently. When he had first informed him in general of the transactions of the monastery, he pressed him to consider seriously that new incidents might arise, new dangers threaten him, which might not always be prevented. He spoke with severity of his irresolute and timid conduct: asked, if it was his purpose to abandon all his glorious hopes, to return disgraced and rejected; to encounter scorn and reproach, as a person unworthy of the regards of this Lady, presumptuous and unjust. Nothing could secure his honour from ruin, or perhaps his life from revenge, but his immediate nuptials with the

Countess. Of this he spoke, as of an event absolutely in the power of Raymond, and delayed only by his mistaken tenderness. He was heard with earnest surprise: but when his Lord began to plead the difficulties he had encountered, and the obstinacy of Ela in denying her consent, he hastily interrupted him.—"Let a day be appointed," cried this minion, "for the celebration of your nuptials, let it be known through the land, let your attendants be ordered to prepare for this event, and your Knights directed to hold themselves in such readiness as the joyful occasion requires.—Let the rest be my care." Raymond, who still preserved a tender affection for the Countess, and remembered with horror how dangerously she had been affected by the insolence of Grey, hesitated, and insisted on a full explanation of this mysterious language. Grey again urged the absolute necessity of prevailing in his present undertaking, both for his honour and his safety; the eternal infamy, nay, the utter impossibility of receding, after having already proceeded thus far. To this he added some artful praises of the Countess, and many animated observations on the happiness of that man who should possess such a treasure of beauty. When the passions of his Lord had by such discourse been raised to the utmost degree of fervour, he began to flatter his hopes: "This Lady," said he, "you at first found reluctant, and no wonder: for she had not been assured that Lord William was really no more. Of this she now seems persuaded, but regards his death as an event too recent, to admit another wooer. What though she hath discovered such impatience of your love? what though she hath attempted to escape from this place? would she not have persevered in her design? would she not have continued her flight, if this reluctance and aversion had not been artfully assumed to give her honour and respect in the general eye? She affects to summon friends to rescue her from your power; but she hopes that they will interpose, and persuade her to accept your hand: but do we delay 'till some new suitor shall arrive, and, under the pretence of relieving the oppressed, and revenging her wrongs, shall successfully court her love, and build his own fortune on your disgrace and ruin?"—Raymond was moved, and seemed ready to pay implicit obedience to the dictates of his creature.—Grey then spoke of the zeal of Reginhald his brother, and his entire devotion to the service of his noble patron. "This faithful Monk," said he, "will be of use. Observe the Countess for some days; continue your fond wooing with all modest and respectful duty, but with unabated zeal. She will soon experience that the flight of Oswald hath not proved effectual to collect her creatures round her: and the disappointment will depress her proud spirit, and convince her that her own and her son's fate still depend on you. The day on which your attendants are taught to expect your nuptials, may perhaps find her consenting to your wishes: but why should we demand or expect her formal consent? Reginhald shall join your hands by virtue of his sacred authority, and pronounce the solemn benediction which shall make her yours forever. Her heart shall secretly applaud this gentle violence. At least, her son, restored to her arms, shall be the purchase of your pardon."—Little of art was required to disguise or palliate the baseness of this design, so effectually had he prepared the mind of Raymond for its reception, by raising the storm of passions to darken and confound his reason. This Lord at once resigned himself to the guidance of his minion, and consented to pursue such measures as he should dictate. The Monk was now summoned before him, and appeared in the most abject abasement and servility. Raymond thanked him for his zeal, promised to repay his services, and ordered him to observe exactly the directions of his brother. Reginhald bowed lowly, and attempted to speak his duty and submission, but in disordered and ungraceful language; then retired with Grey.

These wicked agents, thus invested with full authority, and prompted by their hopes of interest and favour, vigorously pursued the work of oppression and deceit. Reginhald repaired to his monastery (so was he directed by his brother) where he urged the fathers to proceed, without delay, in their obsequies to the deceased Lord, as his widow now prepared, and had appointed a day for her second nuptials, which were only delayed, 'till these religious rites had first been duly performed. The reverend clerks were arrayed in their sacred vestments, and chanted forth the solemn requiem. The neighbouring peasant caught the religious sounds, curiously enquired the cause of these extraordinary devotions, and spread the tidings of the intended marriage through the adjacent country. In the meantime, the attendants and domestics of Raymond were taught to expect the nuptials of their Lord on a day assigned, and ordered to hold them ready for this joyful event. The sound of busy preparation was loud through all the castle, and was heard even to the apartment of the Countess, who wondered, enquired, and was not long a stranger to the cause. She conceived it to be no other than an artifice of her importunate wooer, to deceive the friends of her house, and to destroy the credit of Oswald, her faithful emissary (of whose confinement she was yet uninformed.) With scorn and indignation she reflected on the base attempt to sully her bright fame, and to persuade her friends, that, in defiance of the strict restraints of decent widowhood, and the respect which the memory of a noble husband claimed, she had, within the space of a few months, listened to the solicitations of a new suitor, and consented to receive the hand of her oppressor. If the honour and reverence with which she reflected on Lord William had been somewhat impaired by her suspicions of his disloyalty, a new and more violent aversion to Lord Raymond now possessed her mind, and there still kept up an inflexible resolution never to acknowledge his pretensions to her inheritance, or to accept his love. In such dispositions she received the visits of this Lord with disdain, nor answered his tenders of affection, but by inveighing with all the bitterness of contempt and abhorrence against the mean deceit which he was now practising. Raymond was abashed: he could not deny the accusation, but, with an ill-affected openness, declared that he had indeed assured his friends, that his wishes would be speedily crowned, as he would not suppose that she could forever continue thus unreasonably obdurate, and obstinately insensible to her own happiness.

Such were their interviews; and such the fixed aversion and proud disdain of the Countess, unsubdued by oppression, grief, and fear. Her tedious and melancholy hours were still wasted in alarms for her son, in anxious expectation of relief; of the arrival and vigorous interposition of her friends, and of the defeat and disgrace of her oppressor. In vain did she incessantly enquire, complain, condemn the slow procedure of those who should fly to assert her cause. No messenger of deliverance appeared, no voice of comfort did she receive: but on the morning of that day, which Raymond had presumptuously proclaimed his marriage-day, she still found herself the helpless and joyless prisoner of her false guest.

SECTION IV

Raymond, now on the point of executing his bold purpose, trembled with anxiety, doubt, and solicitude. Grey himself felt an inward agitation, although he laboured to encourage and confirm his Lord. The Monk alone stood stupidly insensible of the importance or of the baseness of the design. The attendants were disposed in their appointed stations; and joy and festivity seemed prepared. The apartments of the Countess alone were sad and solitary, where Elinor was still suffered to perform all kind offices to her afflicted Lady. At the appointed hour, Raymond appeared before her, and first in gentle terms reproached her unkind coldness and severity; but urged his love in a manner more bold and peremptory. She was silent: he renewed his instances: she breathed a deep sigh, and looked up to heaven as if complaining of her unmerited distress, her helpless state, which exposed her to these insolent and hateful solicitations. He seized her hand; she struggled to disengage herself, whilst her eyes darted fiery disdain. In that moment the brothers entered. At sight of Reginhald she shuddered with horror and dismay, though yet unacquainted with the purpose of his appearance. A solemn pause of silence ensued; the Countess trembling; Raymond confounded; and the brothers, who could not behold this disorder without some faint emotion, collecting new force, and arming themselves against the assaults of pity.

An encouraging glance from Grey, at length, emboldened his Lord to break silence. He conjured the Countess by all her hopes of peace, all the tenderness she felt for her darling son, no longer to delay her own happiness; no longer to continue thus perversely insensible of his just pretensions to her love. He now stood before her, he declared, to claim those rights which the royal favour had conferred upon him; that neither his honour, nor his love, permitted him, any longer, to flatter her pride, or to indulge her weak scruples.—She fell upon her knees, and began to utter an earnest and passionate vow, that she never would consent to accept his hand; but Raymond and his associates quickly interrupted and raised her from the ground. Nor was her great spirit yet subdued by this rude violence: she turned upon them with looks of astonishment and disdain. Raymond entreated; Grey reproved her pride; and Reginhald denounced the vengeance of heaven against her obstinacy: whilst the tender mind of Elinor, wounded deeply by the distress of her dear mistress thus surrounded with cruelty and oppression, eased itself in unavailing tears. Raymond still held the hand of Ela; and the impious Monk, who had waited for the signal from Grey, suddenly began to pronounce the marriage rites; but was instantly interrupted by loud and piercing shrieks frequently and violently repeated both by the Countess and her attendant. The unhappy Lady could not long support this violent emotion; she sunk down upon her couch; and Raymond hung over her with a mixture of tenderness and vexation. After a long interval of faint and breathless depression, she seemed to revive, and prepared to speak. Reginhald seized the moment of her recovery, and again began the holy office.—But in that instant a new and unexpected interruption checked his profane purpose, and confounded the base attempt of usurpation and cruel oppression. The sound of haste and trepidation seemed to approach the chamber. Raymond started; the brothers shook at the alarm; a voice was heard calling loudly on Grey. He issued forth; Raymond and the Monk followed: they saw a domestic pale and breathless with haste, who just found words to declare that Lord William was on his way, and would speedily reach the castle.

Not the condemned criminal when he receives his final sentence; not the sinner, yet unconfirmed in guilt, when the sudden crash of thunder appals his spirit, ever shrunk into such abject consternation, as Raymond now experienced from this shocking intelligence. Grey was scarcely less confounded, although he feared only for his safety, and had no sense of wounded honour. They hastened into an adjacent apartment, where Reginhald alone was sufficiently composed to examine this messenger of terror; who informed them, that his appointed duty had led him to some distance from the castle, where he had discovered a small company of travellers, who, on his nearer approach, appeared in disorder and perplexity: that they had demanded his condition and place of residence, and on their part informed him, that they were the attendants and messengers of Lord William, who had landed on the coast of Cornwall, and was soon to resume the possession of his castle: the information they had received on their way of the nuptials of the Countess had filled them with consternation; three of them had resolved to return and convey this intelligence to their Lord, whilst an equal number now hastened forward, if possible, to prevent so fatal a purpose.—"Behold!" said he, pointing downwards from the window which commanded a full view of the castle-gates, "their speed hath equalled mine, and they are now entering."—Grey rushed out, and ordered the domestic to follow. He received the unwelcome guests with an appearance of respect. They were conducted to an apartment, and entertained with due courtesy by the man who had brought the news of their arrival, and who now had strict charge, that for a while they should be kept from any intercourse or conference with the other attendants.

A small ray of hope seemed to dart through the gloom which had possessed the mind of Grey, when he found that Lord William himself was not yet arrived. A little respite seemed of moment, as it allowed him to reflect, and to concert his future measures. At first, he thought of abandoning his Lord, and securing himself by flight; but, although Raymond should not be able to revenge such desertion, the power and resentment of Lord Hubert were terrible, and could not fail to destroy him. Gay hopes of sharing in the riches of this great house of Salisbury, had long possessed his imagination; and he now felt the most implacable hatred of the man who was approaching to defeat these gay hopes. His malice and his fears conspired to recommend the most desperate course of action. He resolved to make one daring effort more, and, if possible, still to establish the pretensions of his master, and to remove his rival by a bold assassination.

In such dispositions did this wicked minion return to his Lord. He found him sunk in despair, and tortured with distraction. Scarcely had he began to speak, when Raymond, starting up in frantic emotion, seized upon him with dreadful menaces of vengeance, as the treacherous murderer of his honour and his peace; and cursed himself and his vile seducer in all the bitterness of remorse. Reginhald fled, and sought to hide himself from the terror of his resentment. Grey, without the least expostulation, the least attempt to allay the fury of his Lord, suffered the violence of passion to take its free course, and to waste its force in fruitless execrations. And soon was the storm allayed; and Raymond, as if recovering from a sudden frenzy, softened into grief and tenderness, condemned his own extravagance, and entreated his favourite to advise, direct, and extricate him from this difficult and dangerous situation.

Grey neither endeavoured to palliate the disgrace, nor to lessen the danger, which his Lord dreaded. He observed that Raymond had indeed proceeded so far as to leave no doubt that he had disregarded the conditions imposed by the King, and had attempted the most lawless acts of oppression. His own part in these transactions he represented as the effects of his unbounded zeal for the service of his master; a zeal which threatened to involve him in the fatal consequences of an injured husband's vengeance. Such discourse only served to irritate the pain which Raymond felt. "Is there no way to retreat with honour?" cried he. "No! nor with safety," returned his minion. "Let us not think of retreat. We are engaged, and must pursue our purpose. You wonder; but the way is obvious, and there is but one way. Perhaps this husband comes but slightly attended: you have Knights and men of arms. Nay, start not. Shall we tamely hold our throats, and receive death from him? No; this arm shall prevent the blow."—Raymond had long been accustomed to resign himself to the guidance of this favourite: by him he had been gradually led on from one excess to the other; and so thoroughly was his mind prepared to receive the very worst impressions, (such is the fatal consequence of the first deviation from virtue) that, instead of trembling at this last proposal, he seemed only solicitous to know the surest means of effecting it.—And, here again, the favourite assumed that superiority which the pliant temper of his Lord and an intimate acquaintance with his weakness and unjust designs had given him. He desired that all future measures should be entrusted to him; that from him the attendants should be directed to receive their orders. Raymond acquiesced, yet not without the utmost anxiety, and most melancholy presages. His retirement was disturbed and painful: all the inhabitants of the castle plainly perceived that something extraordinary had occurred; something to disorder their Lord, and to perplex his designs. The Countess alone felt some degree of comfort: she fondly imputed the sudden retreat of her persecutors to some happy event which the flight of Oswald had produced, some appearance of her friends, or some accounts of their motions. Hence was her harassed mind enabled to recover from the violent shock which it had just now received.

In the meantime, the vigilant and crafty Grey, once more, sought the messengers of Earl William, who by this time were much alarmed at the manner of their reception. He met them with courteous looks, and declared, that the Countess, who was now ill at ease, and could not admit them to her presence, had sent to inform herself particularly of the intelligence which they brought. They related briefly the landing of William, the place of his present residence, and his intention of speedily returning to his own castle. Grey received the account with coldness and affected diffidence: he observed, that "the most positive assurances had been received that Earl William had perished in France; that, if he really was approaching, he must be received with due respect: but, if envy or malice sought to disturb the approaching happiness of Lord Raymond by false intelligence, his power was great, and his resentment would be violent. By his directions, they were for a short time to be strictly guarded, lest they should alarm the minds of his friends by rumours which might possibly prove groundless; if otherwise, a few days would release them."—They gazed upon each other with surprise, but it was in vain to expostulate; they appealed to time to confirm the truth of their declarations: and Grey then proceeded to summon some of the boldest and most zealous of the attendants on Raymond, who were conducted to their Lord, and by him commanded to receive their orders from his favourite, and implicitly to follow his direction.

These commands Grey pretended to explain more fully. He told them, that, from advices lately received, their Lord had good reason to apprehend a false design to drive him from those possessions, which he so justly claimed, and from whence alone he hoped to derive the power of rewarding his faithful followers; that they were to arm themselves with speed, and carefully to guard all the approaches to the castle, against force or treachery. Nor were they slow to express their zeal and cheerful obedience. And now this wicked minion stood prepared at the head of a resolute and well appointed band, to oppose the entrance of Lord William, and to plunge a dagger in his heart.

Long they waited in anxious expectation of their invaders, but in vain; no invaders appeared, no danger threatened them. Grey began indeed to hope that these strangers had been employed to deceive them, and to raise these false alarms for some purpose yet undiscovered; perhaps by some friends of the Countess, who had learned or suspected her present condition. He visited the messengers frequently, insulted them on the appearance of falsehood which their intelligence now seemed to wear; menaced, and endeavoured to terrify them into a confession of the real purpose of their coming. They steadily adhered to their former declarations, and related such circumstances of the fortunes, the dangers, and the arrival of Lord William on the coast of England, as but too plainly demonstrated their truth and integrity. Grey was convinced, but dissembled his conviction. He waited impatiently for the approach of the Earl, but no intelligence could be received; no unusual appearance, no arrival of strange and unexpected visitants, had broke in upon the silence and tranquillity of the adjacent lands. The disappointment served but the more to perplex and alarm him: his vigilance was not relaxed; he kept his force collected about him, and still stood resolved to meet his danger, and confirmed in his bloody purpose.

Book V

SECTION I

The three faithful followers of Earl WILLIAM, who had determined to return to their Lord, found him just issuing forth from the hall of Randolph, at the head of a small body of attendants. At sight of them his mind was filled with sad presages. He turned upon his ancient friend with surprise: then both rushed forward, impatient to learn the cause of this unexpected return; and instantly received the melancholy tidings, that, whilst their companions had brought the news of the Earl's arrival to the castle of Salisbury, they had returned to acquaint him, that the Countess had given her hand to Raymond, and that his nuptials had been solemnised on the very day of their approach.

The bitterness of this intelligence was too great even for the great soul of WILLIAM. He sunk into a silent dismay, and seemed unwilling or unable to contend with despair. The Knight, whose suspecting thoughts had been prepared for this account, strove to rouse and comfort him, but a long time were his efforts fruitless. The afflicted Lord scarcely forced out, at long and heavy intervals, some broken sighs, some confused and imperfect expressions, of anguish, of resentment, at the supposed unkindness of his wife, and the weakness and unworthiness of her fatal compliance. At length, suddenly starting from this extreme of depression to that of the most violent fury, he uttered dreadful denunciations of vengeance against the destroyer of his peace, and called on his friends to attend him instantly to his castle, and to assist him in a brave and just revenge. But here the caution of the old Knight interposed, and with difficulty prevailed on him to return to his friendly roof, and there to consult maturely upon the most prudent measures. The Earl obeyed, yet seemed intent only on the most violent and daring course. In vain did Randolph remind him of the insufficient numbers of his retinue, and the superior advantages of the usurper. The storm of passion was still loud and terrible; nor could the Earl listen to danger or difficulty: the injuries which his honour had sustained were the sole object of his thoughts, and revenge his sole purpose.

The fair Jacqueline soon perceived a confusion and disorder arising from some unexpected incident; and, impatient to learn the cause, appeared before her host and her protector. Randolph accosted and entreated her to unite her gentle persuasion, and to prevent Lord William from rushing precipitately on ruin. "No!" cried the Earl, hastily interrupting him, "the attempt is not rash, nor the purpose desperate. What though my wife hath so soon forgotten me? What though the absence of a few months was too great for her impatience? What though she hath accepted a second husband? Have my numerous dependants too been false? Have they forgotten me? No! let us collect them! let us fire their brave spirits to revenge their injured Lord; and let his fury fall with its due force upon this adulterous pair."—Jacqueline seemed lost in confusion: Randolph again interposed, and urged the danger of venturing, thus weakly attended, to seek his vassals, and openly to give defiance to Raymond. But now the noble maid recovered from her first surprise, and her great soul began to beam forth through all her virgin reserve. "Where is that power and influence," said she, "in the court of England, which Lord William boasted? If his own wrongs cannot there find redress, if he must have recourse to the precarious chance of arms, in vain have I sought relief in this strange land; in vain have I indulged the pleasing hopes of regaining my lost inheritance, and (if he still supports the miseries of oppression) my injured parent. Will not the King protect"—"He shall give me justice," cried William: "This arm raised him to the throne: this arm can tear him from it." Then embracing her with a paternal fondness, "The spirit of thy brave father," said he, "dwells in thee. Yes, fair partner of my fortunes, the King shall give me justice. Let my wife, no, the wife of Raymond, now enjoy for a while her foul disloyalty. My vengeance shall be first directed against the great author of my wrongs, the proud Hubert. In the face of his misguided Sovereign, before the gallant Nobles of England, will I proclaim his baseness, and demand full redress. Let us hasten to the royal presence: there shall my friends crowd round me, and my vassals attend my orders."

Randolph was pleased at this resolution, which William considered as the most honourable, but he as the safest course. The time, the manner, and all the circumstances of their departure were now settled with more temper and composed deliberation. The Knight insisted to accompany his noble friend, together with his band of followers: Jacqueline consented still to reside in Cornwall, until the Earl had obtained, first, the full redress of his own injuries, and, then, the happy means of rescuing her father, or of revenging his fate. The little troop was soon prepared to enter on their march, and soon took their way, with no ungallant show. The mind of Lord William was still gloomy and disordered. He thought on his wife: the tenderness of her former love, the noble nature which all her actions had invariably displayed, recurred to his mind, but now served only to aggravate his despair. Her strange and precipitate compliance with the desires of Raymond was perplexing: to be so soon forgotten was tormenting: and ever and anon he unbosomed his distracted thoughts to the friendly Knight.

"Foolish and wretched is the man" (thus would he exclaim) "who builds his happiness on the frail and instable affection of woman. O my friend! how securely did I conceive our loves to have been founded! how firmly did her heart seem linked to mine! Can I forget the time, when all the noble youth of England courted the smiles of the rich and beautiful heiress of Earl Patrick, when her eyes marked me out as their most worthy object, and her love graced my rising fame? Can I forget the day when I was first, publicly, distinguished by her favour? The solemn jousts were prepared: the Knights glittered in their pompous array: we were surrounded with all the beauties of the land; but our thoughts and desires were fixed on Ela. How did I labour to engage her attention by my gorgeous entry? Well do I remember the device which then adorned my shield, and which my youthful pride had dictated. It was an eagle towering in air, with his eyes fixed on the sun; and these words beneath: NOT ARROGANT, BUT CONSCIOUS OF NOBLENESS. We traversed the lists in solemn state; and each champion, as he passed, made low obeisance towards the place where Ela sat; but each unnoticed, 'till, William pacing proudly by, and paying the just homage to her high beauty, suddenly she let fall the knot of ribbons which adorned her lovely arm. I seized, kissed, and fixed it in my crest: and on that day did my gallant deeds confess my zeal to merit her high regards. Many a spear was bravely shivered: but, e're our appointed courses were finished, a loud and sudden shriek assailed our affrighted ears: we turned and saw the scaffold, where this fair dame was seated, yielding to its load. I burst like lightning to her rescue; and, amidst all the officious and vigorous interposition of the crowd, which the dangerous incident had collected, this arm it was which saved her.—And did our loves decrease? Was my heart ever estranged? Was it one moment seduced to any other object?—And yet, so soon to be forgotten! the false tidings of my death so eagerly received!"—

Randolph was studious to divert him from this melancholy subject. Revenge, he knew, was grateful to the high soul of William; and he laboured to inspire him with hopes of a brave revenge. He spoke of the arts that had been used to influence the weakness of a widowed, unfriended, unassisted woman; of the craft of Hubert, and his iniquitous abuse of the royal favour. "But now," said he, "the King shall know this minion: he shall know with what malicious purpose of oppression and injustice his false heart conceived, and his false tongue uttered the lying tale of Earl William's death; and speedily shall he execute the full vengeance due to the wounded honour of his brave kinsman."—With eyes darting indignation, and sounds of disdain, the Earl replied, that his own influence and reputation in England, his noble friends and numerous adherents, had made kings; and that he relied on these much more than on the justice of young Harry. "Alas," said he, "little can thy honest heart conceive of that craft and wily insinuation with which this courtier hath wound himself to the heart of his easy prince. He alone directs and commands him. The noblest spirits of England are insolently scorned; and the remotest corner of the realm feels his pernicious influence." "Good heaven," cried Randolph (still labouring to divert the Earl from the gloomy subject which lay deeply fixed in his mind, and was ever ready to rise and torment him), "When shall our distracted country feel the blessings of a wise and virtuous rule? Shall faction and tumult forever disturb the land, and sordid avarice and slavish adulation forever surround the throne? Is the insolence of ill-gotten power to know no control? Sad and gloomy is the prospect!—And, yet, the spirits of my brave countrymen, though depressed and overborne, are still unbroken. They have already contended, and they may again contend for the great prize of freedom. Perhaps (and truly pleasing it is to indulge that hope) England may yet experience some happy age, when wisdom, and valour, and virtue shall conspire to bless and to exalt her. Some glorious Monarch may yet hold her imperial sceptre, flourishing in all the pride of youth, loved and revered by his grateful people, and dreaded by the enemies of justice and his kingdom. Perhaps the pious care of some illustrious parent may have formed his mind to all princely virtues; perhaps some noble friend of exalted merit and unsullied integrity may have aided the glorious work. Wisdom and justice may guide his councils, and valour lead forth his victorious armies: the united voice of a happy people may bless him, and the united force of all his enemies may sink before him. If heaven should be thus gracious to our country, could its transcendent favour admit of any accession?—Yes! let the happiness, diffused from the throne, be reflected back on such a Monarch. Let him be amply rewarded, in a princely consort, fitted to grace his royal seat, and relieve his generous cares.—Then, let the ardent prayers of his people be accepted. Let the princely pair flourish, and very late pay the debt of nature: from heir to heir let their virtues be transmitted; and immortal be the glories and blessings of their reign!"

The spirit of the good Knight was elevated and inflamed by this idea of public felicity, the most exalted and complete which his imagination could form: and William seemed to forget his private grief, and to be wrapt in the same pleasing dream. And now they approached towards the city of Marlborough where Henry still held his court. The distant view of this royal seat raised a violent agitation in the breast of Salisbury. He was now on the point of breaking from his obscurity, and once more shining forth in his native sphere: and he felt all the emotion of an high and noble mind, impatient of wrongs, ready to urge them boldly, and resolute to seek redress. He entered the city, when suddenly his spirit was still farther agitated by a strange and unexpected encounter. A small, but gallant, troop approached him, headed by a youth of noble port. Their leader had already fixed his eyes upon him, with marks of wonder; and, stopping, as if deprived of all power of motion, pronounced the name of Salisbury. William came forward with courteous demeanour, attentively surveying the stranger, who at once ended his suspense, yet increased his wonder, by declaring himself the young Lord of Poictiers, that Chauvigny whom his generosity had restored to an injurious father. A sudden exclamation of surprise burst from the Earl, and an interval of silence ensued: at length he was enabled to exclaim—"Good heavens! the son of the oppressor and murderer of my friend!—And in England!—The father too, perhaps, is ready to insult our wrongs, and boast of his perfidious cruelty."—"With his ashes," replied the youth, "let his errors also lie buried. Dost thou love the good Les Roches? He is my friend and father: extend thy love to me, and say, bless me with the happy tidings, that the fair Jacqueline hath escaped the storm of contention and misfortune, and lives in safety."—"Would to heaven!" cried the Earl, "that her father were now in England, to embrace and bless her; to be witness of her noble nature, and to thank the saints for her preservation!"—The young Lord could no longer restrain his impatient ardour; they had both alighted, and he now rushed on Earl William, and clung round his neck, with all the extravagance of joy. "What though," said he, "the brave Les Roches be still pursued by the severity of fortune; he may be rescued; he may be yet restored to honour and happiness: Lord William will not deny his assistance; he will aid me with his power, whilst I labour to restore him!"—"Now," cried the Earl, "I am indeed thy friend.—But we are at the English court. Here must I make a trial of my power. If the name of Salisbury be not forgotten; if a few months of obscurity have not totally effaced the remembrance of my birth, my actions, and my services, I shall yet obtain redress of my private wrongs; and, if he still survives, I shall relieve my friend."

Thus saying, he rushed forward, with an aspect of fiery resentment and indignation. Chauvigny turned back with his followers, and attended him, expecting some important discovery, some explanation of what the Earl had hastily and obscurely hinted. They soon reached the very centre of greatness and magnificence; and, now, the long lost Earl of Salisbury once more appeared in becoming state amidst the Nobles of England, shining like the great light of heaven when just emerged from a dark and baleful eclipse. His ancient friends embraced him; his peers crowded round him, impatient to learn the story of his wonderful deliverance. Not so the crafty Hubert: he heard of his arrival with terror, and beheld him with confusion and dismay. The young King hastened to congratulate his noble kinsman, who sunk upon his knee, loudly calling for justice and redress. Henry raised him, and demanded the cause and purpose of his petition. The Earl collected his great spirit, and, with looks of terror and disdain, pointed to Hubert, whilst silence and suspense possessed the crowd of nobles. "Come forth," said he, "thou wicked author of my wrongs! come forth, and meet the vengeance due to thy treachery.—Here stands the wretched caitiff, (such this arm shall prove him) who basely seized the fatal moment of my absence to destroy my peace and happiness forever. Bear witness for me, ye warlike Barons and Nobles of this land, with what zealous loyalty I laboured to support the cause of Henry, and to establish our rightful King on that royal seat: for him and for our country have I encountered the toils and desperate calamities of war, the fury of proud foes and formidable hosts, the rage of storms and waves, and the dangers of the tempestuous ocean. Scarcely have these shattered limbs supported the painful task of honour, and wonderful hath my deliverance been. And what is my recompense? Whilst I fought in Gascoigne, this pernicious courtier, who never experienced the hazards and distresses of the field, never knew aught but the luxurious ease of a palace, contrived the ruin of the brave harassed soldier. He chose out his minion, his nephew, the unworthily-ennobled Raymond: he filled the royal ears with false and malicious tales of my death; he sent his creature to seize my castle, my power, and my extended domain; and to insult my unhappy Countess with his adulterous love: he hath abused her weakness; he hath deceived her credulity, or perhaps by force possessed himself of her bed. I seek not for reparation: my wrongs will not admit of this; but I call for just punishment, for vengeance due to that deadly wound my honour hath thus sustained. To the justice of my liege Lord I fly,—to your royal justice, rather than to the influence which Salisbury still maintains, and the power which he still commands in England."

Henry was embarrassed and disordered by the boldness of this address. The precipitation with which he had yielded to the desires of Hubert now appeared in the true light, and covered him with confusion. He prepared to accost the Earl in such soothing terms as he could command in this disorder of his thoughts, when the favourite, versed in all the refined arts of dissimulation, hastily prevented him, and thus assumed the semblance of a generous impatience of all censure or suspicion:

"That I rejoice at the happy arrival of Earl William, the saints are witnesses: that I believed him dead surely cannot be deemed a crime, when such repeated assurances were received that he had shared the fate of his unhappy countrymen. What though I too indulgently consented to the wishes of my nephew, and obtained him permission to woo the gentle Countess, whom all the land regarded as a widow? What force, what fraud, what injury was meditated? What injustice hath been committed? What vile dishonest purposes have been pursued, that vengeance is so loudly denounced? The soul of Raymond is noble, and his procedure hath been honourable. True, he sought the Countess; he found her deep in sorrow; he indulged her sorrow; nor urged his passion with the importunity of violent love. He waited, if, happily, time and his tender cares might move the Countess to listen to his suit; but, thanks to the interposing providence of heaven, his suit could not prevail.—Go, Lord William, repair to thy princely castle: there thy wife waits to receive thee; there shalt thou find her unassailed and unpolluted. Go, and be happy; and, when thou reflectest on thine own credulity, learn to forgive those who too easily received the false story of thy death."

The Earl gazed in silence, doubting, yet willing to believe these happy tidings. Hubert repeated his assurances with an aspect steady and composed. "By my Holidame!" exclaimed the King, "it rejoiceth us that Lord William hath now found his suspicions false: not the unexpected deliverance and happy arrival of our noble cousin give us greater joy.—But let us forget all jealousies, and despise all false rumours.—Embrace, and forgive Lord Hubert, command our power, and enjoy the rewards of thy gallant toils."—The courtiers echoed the sentiments of their Prince, and William with a constrained submission gave his hand to Hubert: his noble friends were collected round him, and renewed their congratulations: the King by his caresses seemed willing to efface the remembrance of that easiness with which he had yielded to the desires of his favourite, and this favourite, by an assumed affection and humbleness of deportment, sought to quench all remains of animosity in the mind of the injured Earl; but conscious of his own artifice and hypocrisy, he naturally suspected that readiness of belief, with which Salisbury seemed to yield to his declarations, as well as that sudden calm of peace and reconciliation, in which his fury appeared to subside. He had injured, and therefore hated him: he had affirmed boldly to divert the present storm; but, whether the Countess had already yielded to Raymond, or whether he had forcibly possessed himself of her bed, as yet he knew not: and possibly Lord William might detect his falsehood, and return with double fury, to urge his wrongs, and seek his just vengeance. Such thoughts he revolved for a while in his busy mind; and then confirmed himself in the dreadful purpose of concealing his baseness, and providing effectually for his safety and power by the immediate destruction of this Lord.

Far other thoughts now employed the Earl. He had by slow degrees, and by the repeated arts of refined and steady hypocrisy, been wrought into a firm persuasion, that Hubert had declared the truth; that his messengers had been deceived; and that his wife still preserved her loyalty: and he freely indulged these delightful thoughts, which naturally inspired an enlivened joy and complacency. The gracious condescensions of the King he received with just returns of duty; he shared in the delight which his noble friends expressed at his return; and, although he wondered, yet was he affected with due pleasure, at the zeal and love which the young Lord of France discovered, at that earnestness of friendship which seemed so kindly interested in his fortunes. But not the splendour and pleasures of a court, not the affection of friends, nor the smiles of royal favour, could detain him in the city of Marlborough. He was impatient to seek his own noble mansion, and his attendants held themselves in readiness to accompany him. Without any delay, but what refreshment necessarily demanded, he took a dutiful leave of the King; he received the repeated assurances of Hubert, that his nephew had already retired from the castle, and that the Countess waited to embrace him with unabated love; and he departed at the head of his little troop, now reinforced by the followers of Lord Chauvigny, who declared his resolution to attend the Earl of Salisbury.

They took their way; and William, who had hitherto been totally engaged by his own great affairs, was now more at ease, and more at leisure to recall the tender sentiments of friendship, and to think on the good Les Roches. "Gentle Lord," said he addressing himself to young Chauvigny, "how have I deserved this zealous attachment, these extraordinary instances of your affection? Say, what surprising events have brought thee hither? Say, how hath Les Roches merited those tender names, I think thou gavest him, of friend and father? What of his fortunes canst thou inform me? If he indeed survives, where shall I seek him? How shall I restore his daughter?"—The mention of Jacqueline brightened the countenance of her lover with a momentary joy, which was instantly clouded, and with a sigh which awakened all the fears of William, he exclaimed at the severity with which fortune had pursued his generous friend. "I still hope," said he, "and on that hope rests all my comfort, that he is now in England, but whither driven, or where he may now lay his melancholy head, alas, I know not. It is my purpose to seek him, and in this good purpose Earl William surely must assist me.—Let me unfold the story of our fortunes, and no longer wonder to see Chauvigny in this land."—They rode slowly on apart from their associates, all but the good old Knight; and the Frenchman thus began.

SECTION II

"How can I reflect on that credulity, with which my father yielded to the false and malicious representations of Mal-leon, and that unmerited severity with which he pursued our generous friend?—Peace and forgiveness to his departed spirit!—If thou hast already heard how the hunted fugitive ranged through the wilds and desert mountains, spare me the odious recital: yes, thou must have heard. Thy brave countrymen, who long defended him, must have at length found their Lord. Their valour only could have rescued thee from the snares of envy and cruelty. And may due honour and reward attend that fidelity, which guarded the unhappy devoted head of Les Roches! Long time they watched over him in his melancholy retreat: nor was it their want of vigilance, but his own absence of thought and careless inattention to danger, which at last separated him from their protection.

"It was on the morning of a night of broken and disordered slumbers, that the unhappy Lord started from his hard couch, full of inward grief and agitation. The woody covert where he had sought repose, at first, concealed his motions from the Englishmen, who watched at some distance. Insensibly was he led on, wrapt up in sad and painful reflection; and wandered solitary down the winding path, which led from the mountain, was divided, and gradually lost in a vale encumbered with shrubs and rocks, and watered by a resounding current. At length he awakened as from a dream, stared round on the aweful prospect, and sought to gain his companions. But, alas! he had wandered too far, and too incautiously. Perplexed and confounded, encompassed with steep hills, which the luxuriant hand of nature had clothed with a wild magnificence of forest; and, ever and anon, diverted from his course by the rocky fragments which the torrent seemed to have washed down into the valley; his eyes searched in vain for the path which he had taken: he hasted on, and paused by turns, without direction, nor totally free from terror; when suddenly he descried a venerable personage, clad in the habit of austere piety, on which the silver beard descended from a grave and emaciated visage. The hermit advanced, raising his shrivelled hands in holy benediction over our astonished friend; and, as Les Roches bowed before him, he enquired with surprise what fate or chance had led him into this rude and solitary retreat.

"The afflicted Lord, awed by his reverend aspect, yet comforted by that benevolence which beamed forth from his looks, and softened all his accents, freely acknowledged that he was the wretched child of calamity, driven to the desert by persecution and oppression; and that he sought the neighbouring hills, where a few friends, they too sharers in his misfortune, waited his return. The reverend father, who saw his anguish, comforted, exhorted, and by degrees so far gained on his confidence, that he freely acknowledged his name and quality, and briefly related the events which had driven him from the society of men. The hermit was moved, and, pointing to his cell, which lay at no great distance, 'There,' said he, 'shall thou find refuge, 'till these storms of calamity have wasted their violence. Come on, my son, enter and partake of my homely refreshment: your friends too shall be my care. Tarry here: I know all the windings and secret paths of these unfrequented hills. I shall soon find them: and here shall they enjoy a more secure, and, perhaps, less uncomfortable retreat.' The Baron made obeisance, and accepted the generous invitation. The hermit laboured up the precipice with slow and painful steps, towards the place which Les Roches had described. But here he found no unhappy strangers: all was silence and solitude. He returned full of fears and sad forebodings, which his tenderness of nature had dictated. He entered his cave, but this too was silent and solitary: no guest appeared; no afflicted Lord waited his arrival.

"However cautiously Les Roches had directed his course, however secret and retired he had chosen his residence, still had his motions been long watched by some base and ignoble men, allured by the rewards promised to those who should discover and seize him. Four sordid hinds, disguised in the garb of wood-men, had diligently traced him through all his various progress, but still were terrified and kept at wary distance by the vigilance and well known valour of his attendants. The moment of his separation had not escaped them: they exulted, and resolved to seize this critical occasion. They pursued his steps, and hastened down to the valley by different routes to them well known. They lay unnoticed, impatient to snatch their prey: they marked the late conference, and saw the hermit depart; and no sooner was he lost in the distant wood, than rushing furiously into the cave, and drawing their concealed weapons, they seized the unhappy Lord unprepared for resistance. In vain did he enquire the cause, and endeavour to expostulate: they sternly commanded him to attend their pleasure, and, hurrying him precipitately away, directed their course towards the castle of Poictiers, filled with the delightful idea of those rewards they were to receive for a service so important. Their victim attended them, patient and resigned to their insolence, disdaining all entreaties and complaints; and was at length conducted into our hall, as a man indifferent to his fate, and prepared boldly to meet the worst that oppression could inflict.

"But here he found a strange and unlooked for reception; and all the sanguine hopes of his sordid hunters were lost in confusion and disgrace. Fortunately some followers of Les Roches, who had been made prisoners, and were examined by my father, distinctly recounted the events in the Isle of Rhè, and fired his brave spirit with indignation and contempt for the Count Mal-leon. He began to lament the precipitate and misguided severity with which he had pursued our friend, and to revere the character of Lord Salisbury. In that moment he received the account of my flight, with true paternal grief and anxiety. His joy at my speedy return was equally extravagant; and soon was he informed of the generosity that restored me to his arms. Alas! these violent and repeated impressions were too great for his weak and disordered frame. He had long been oppressed by a dangerous malady, which, as it had inflamed and irritated his spirit to an unusual degree of impatience and fretful violence, so was it, in return, inflamed and irritated by the events which this violence had produced. Too late did he lament his fatal rashness, and utter his ineffectual wishes to make a full atonement. On the very morning when Les Roches arrived at Poictiers, we were alarmed with the symptoms of his dissolution, and in these arms did he expire.

"Too intent on paying the mournful offices to my deceased parent, I could scarcely give a thought to Les Roches; I had just the power to issue my command that he should be treated nobly. Thus did he continue for some time a prisoner, unnoticed, and uncertain of his fate: an interval which we afterwards lamented bitterly. To that we imputed the loss of Jacqueline; to that, the distresses of Lord William; which our imaginations represented in the most frightful form, all derived from my unhappy delay in seeking and offering him protection. At length the remains of Lord Chauvigny were interred with all solemn rites befitting his exalted condition. I now became Lord of his power and domain, and soon found leisure to think on the father of my beloved Jacqueline. The hinds who had made him my prisoner, and now applied for their reward, saw me fall at his feet and embrace him, with all the rapture of affection and reverence. They would gladly have made a merit of preserving and conveying him to my castle: nor should I have denied their reward, but that their rude insolence had aggravated the distresses of my friend. I instantly pronounced him free; I vowed to devote all my influence and power, to make atonement for his unmerited sufferings; to exert the most zealous efforts of love and friendship to regain his daughter and to relieve Lord Salisbury. But these efforts were exerted too late. Les Roches was indeed re-instated in full possession of his lands and castle: but, not all our most diligent enquiries, not all our vigilance and labour in traversing the wildest and most unfrequented parts of our province, could obtain the least information of his daughter, or his friend; so secretly had Salisbury chosen his retreat:—or perhaps he was then contending with storms and waves: perhaps securely landed on his own native shore. This last thought was pleasing, and we were inclined to indulge it.

Thus while my breast was filled with all the impatience of love, and paternal fondness equally predominant in Les Roches, we soon concurred in the adventurous resolution of seeking the dear treasure in England, which fortune had so unkindly torn from us. Thither, said we, hath Jacqueline been conducted by her noble protector, and there shall we find both utterly despairing to regain Les Roches. Inflamed with such hopes, we instantly prepared our retinue, a gay and gallant train: we soon reached the coast, and soon were we embarked: alas, too soon! little suspecting the severe reverse of fortune that now threatened to confound all our flattering expectations.

"The sea was rough and stormy; our barque stout and amply furnished, but our mariners were unskilful; and long time did we contend with all the violence of the winds, and long time were we driven from our destined course. And when at last, after various dangers and difficulties, we were cheered with the hopes of speedily gaining the English coast, suddenly we found ourselves assailed by a bold piratical vessel, and threatened with a severe captivity. The hostile intentions of our adversary were but too plainly discovered, as he bore down upon us. Our force was instantly collected, and we resolved to defend our liberty with due spirit. Tortured at the thought of being prevented from pursuing my design, I raved in all the wildness of frenzy and desperation, which the good Les Roches endeavoured to restrain, himself equally resolute, but inspired with a more deliberate and rational courage. No sooner had the enemy closed with us, than this gallant Lord, earnest to prevent me in the pursuit of danger, leaped on board his vessel, was followed by a few attendants, and there maintained a bloody and unequal conflict. We pressed forward, earnest to second this bold attack; the pirate was alarmed at our numbers and our resolution, when, suddenly, the violence of the surge separated our vessels; and as we endeavoured to regain our former station, anxious for the rescue of our companions, we were shocked with the view of the pirate flying before us. His vessel was of quicker sail, and his mariners more expert. He left us in rage and anguish, uttering fruitless execrations, and straining our limbs in fruitless efforts to regain our captive friends. In the bitterness of grief and disappointment, I resolved to continue the pursuit, if happily some favourable incident might bring the enemy once more into our reach; and for a while the pursuit was continued. But the storm was loud, and my followers too sensible of their danger. They forced me to make towards land; and, after much hazard and difficulty, we were at length disembarked on the southern coast of England.

"We recounted our late adventure to the inhabitants of the coast, who well knew the pirate we described, and had oftentimes suffered by his depredations. They informed us that his name was William de Morisco, a bold adventurer, who had of late frequently infested their dwellings, and probably, e're long, might alarm them by another descent: that his exactions had ever been severe, but that his nature, rude as it was, discovered no wanton cruelty, no malicious thirst for blood; that an honourable ransom might prevail upon him to set our friends at liberty. I was comforted by this intelligence, and waited for a time, in hopes of some favourable opportunity of recovering Les Roches: but no vessel appeared; no intelligence was received.

"Unable to support this delay, I resolved once more to seek the enemy at sea. My followers I knew would prove averse to such an attempt; and the occasion demanded more skilful mariners, and a vessel more completely appointed than ours, which by this time had felt the severity of winds and seas. I therefore formed the bold design of applying for assistance directly at the English court. A young King, jealous of his honour, could not be unmoved at the insults offered to his territory by this obscure adventurer: he must readily favour the generous purpose of pursuing and engaging him: and, if Lord Salisbury hath now regained his native country, he cannot be less zealous to rescue his friend; he must effectually aid my endeavours.—Thus I reasoned; and, leaving a part of my retinue on the coast to treat for the ransom of our friends, if the pirate should appear, I proceeded to the court of England, where jousts and tournaments were prepared for the entertainment of the King, now recovering from a tedious sickness. In these I engaged; nor was I disgraced, or my attendants unnoticed. Henry vouchsafed his attention to the stranger, and received me with a princely welcome. I called myself a young Lord of one of those provinces of France that acknowledged the English jurisdiction; and declared the whole story of my adventure on the voyage towards England. The King was duly affected with indignation, commended the gallant resolution I expressed of seeking the pirate, and readily promised to entrust the chastisement of this insolent plunderer to my command.

"Lord Hubert, whom I soon found to be principal in the confidence of his master, echoed the sentiments of Henry: he frequently held converse with me, and enquired much about the affairs of my province. Discourse of the late wars naturally introduced the name of Salisbury: I sighed, and Hubert hastily demanded if I could say aught of the fortunes of this Lord. The melancholy air which I assumed, redoubled his attention: I told him that Lord William had landed in France, had been pursued by the fury of his unjust enemies, fled with a noble maid whose father had deeply shared in his calamities; and, since he was not by this time returned to his native country, I feared for both.—Hubert, with an impatience and violence to me unaccountable, hastily interrupted me, by declaring that William must have perished; and this delivered in a tone and manner which indicated too plainly, that he felt a peculiar pleasure in this persuasion. I was alarmed; I cautiously avoided all farther explanation, and coldly assented to his opinion: but Hubert, naturally jealous, and practised in the arts and policy of courts, suspected my silence. He was sensible that I had suppressed some part of my story: he treated me with distance and reserve, and my suit sped but coldly. Frequently did I remind him of the royal promise I had received, and urged him to issue the orders necessary for enabling me to seek the pirate. I was long tortured with delays, 'till, quite wearied out by the insincerity of a minister, who interposed like a baleful cloud between me and the favour of his prince, I sought a convenient hour, and once more kneeled to young Henry. He graciously directed me to repair to the coast without farther delay, and at the same time commanded that a vessel should be there prepared, ready to receive and to acknowledge me commander. I bowed, and kissed the royal hands: I collected my attendants:—I met Lord William."

"In a happy hour!" replied the Earl:—"but, gentle Lord, be not diverted from thy purpose: haste thou to the coast, I shall but visit my castle, and straight follow thee, if happily we may yet recover our noble friend. Jacqueline shall receive us at our joyful return, and thank thee for her father."

SECTION III

Chauvigny prepared to answer, when their conference was suddenly interrupted by the approach of a stranger, who, with gentle aspect and deportment, addressed himself to Salisbury, and kindly congratulated his safe return to England. The Earl beheld him with surprise tempered with due courtesy, and, e're he could demand his name, the stranger observed with earnestness that the dampy shades of night were approaching fast; and pointing to a fair dwelling, which lay at some small distance, invited the Lords to accept of residence and refreshment under his roof, 'till morning. "There," said he, "shall your retinue be also entertained; and there shall Lord William receive some pleasing intelligence from the castle of Salisbury."— Without farther hesitation or enquiry, the Earl joyfully accepted this invitation, and, pressing forward as his host directed, entered a goodly hall, which seemed decked and prepared for his hospitable reception.

Little did this Lord conceive of the danger which now awaited him; of the desperate purposes of Raymond and his associates, and the secret malignity of Hubert, who for some time had entertained a design against his life, and hesitated only about the means of execution. Conscious of the vengeance due to his own baseness and falsehood, and firmly determined to prevent it, he revolved many different schemes of destroying Earl William either by force or fraud. In the midst of such bloody thoughts he was surprised by the arrival of a messenger from Lord Raymond, who desired a private conference: Raymond and his wicked minion had for some time been perplexed and confounded. The intelligence of the three English men (whom they still kept under restraint) was clear and explicit: they adhered invariably to their first account, and frequently repeated their declarations with an ingenuous appearance of truth, wondering that their Lord was not yet arrived. On the other hand, Salisbury did not appear; no farther intelligence was received, no discoveries made by those sent out to watch his approach. In this suspense and uncertainty, Raymond, whose mind was too violently agitated to suggest any calm and deliberate counsels, and Grey, whose wiles seemed to be at length exhausted, concurred in the expediency of dispatching an emissary to Lord Hubert, to inform him of their situation, and to desire his direction. Reginhald was appointed for this purpose, and recommended as a person in whom Hubert might confide. The Monk now appeared before him, and delivered his letters; (having already received the dreadful intelligence that William was now safe in the town of Marlborough.) The piercing eye of Hubert, long used to scan the countenances of men, and there to read their thoughts, narrowly surveyed the aspect of Reginhald, and formed too just conceptions of his temper and disposition. He enquired particularly into the measures his nephew had pursued; and the Monk answered to his questions in such a manner as admitted Hubert to a thorough knowledge of his wicked heart. Fully persuaded that he now had a proper instrument of his deadly purpose, he dismissed the Monk for a while, and appointed an hour for a second conference.

The dark design he now meditated required still some farther assistance. A man there was at this time attendant on the court, whom the crafty minister had frequently made the agent of his oppression and injustice. He had oftentimes sent him out to harass the land by severe and fraudulent exactions, and had suffered him to be enriched by a share of the spoil. Tyrrel (so was he named) lived but by the favour of Hubert, who reserved him for his wicked purposes; yet might at once take away his life with a fair semblance of public justice, should he at any time rebel against his sovereign pleasure. This man was now summoned before him; and, with a brow of care and anxiety, as if some design of moment possessed his mind, Hubert commanded him instantly to repair to his house, which lay near the road Lord William was to take, to invite this Lord; to entertain him with all hospitable rites; and, in some other matters which should hereafter be explained more fully, to submit entirely to the guidance of a Monk whom he should speedily send to him, and whom he was also to entertain. Tyrrel was alarmed at this mysterious language: he knew the desperate unrelenting spirit of his master, and suspected that some bloody design was now to be executed; and that his house was to be the fatal scene of violence or treachery. He trembled and hesitated, for he was not yet consummate in villainy: but Hubert thundered in his ears the most terrible denunciations of vengeance and utter destruction, should he betray the least reluctance, the smallest defect of zeal and alacrity in executing his orders. Tyrrel bowed before him with a slavish submission, and promised full obedience.

Still he had to practise with Reginhald; but here he expected, and indeed found an easy task. The Monk was again summoned to his presence. The distinction and apparent confidence with which he was treated, served to intoxicate his base mind, and to prepare him for some deed of violence or mischief: Hubert artfully commended his fidelity, and promised to reward it, but lamented the danger in which Raymond and all his adherents were now to be involved. Lord William, he observed, must soon reach his castle; the shame of disappointment and the violence of hatred and revenge must soon fall on Raymond; and the zeal of his faithful friends must appear odious and criminal. Then, with well-affected perplexity and terror addressing himself earnestly to the Monk, he desired his sage counsel in this dangerous emergency. Reginhald, with an awkward and abject abasement, declared that he was totally unable to advise, but ready to follow the directions of Lord Hubert with implicit submission. The subtle courtier seized him by the hand, applauded his zeal, lavished the amplest promises upon him. "Be bold," said he, "and be happy.— There is but one way—Let us prevent the attempts of our common enemy—by destroying him."—Reginhald took fire at this proposal: he at once freely offered himself to be the agent, and seemed impatient to learn the means of executing a design so suited to a heart that never felt humanity or remorse.

Hubert hastily produced a phial filled with a deadly poison. "Behold," said he, "the sure means of destroying our enemy. Let it be thy care to present Lord William with this fatal draught, and name the reward of so great a service."—And now he proceeded to explain his fell purpose to the Monk more particularly. He dismissed him fully instructed, and impatient for the execution. Reginhald was received by the abject creature of Hubert, and invested with absolute authority over his domestics; Tyrrel watched the approach of Lord William; this Lord accepted his insidious invitation; and the Monk was brought before him, as a person from whom he was to receive some particular intelligence of his Countess. The Earl was earnest in his enquiries, and Reginhald prompt in his false assurances. He declared (as he had been instructed by Hubert) that he had for some time resided in the castle of Salisbury, employed in administering spiritual consolation to a domestic of the Countess; that he had frequently seen this Lady, been witness of the melancholy of her widowed state, and of the affection with which she cherished the memory of her Lord. A suitor indeed had visited her; but she had obstinately shut her ears against all his solicitations; and Lord Raymond was long since retired in despair.

These studied falsehoods had all the effect for which they were intended. The heart of William was dilated with joy: he embraced his friends with that warmth of affection which sudden good fortune naturally excites: then, turning again to Reginhald, repeated his eager enquiries about his wife, his son, his house; and received such answers as confirmed his joy. He now secretly condemned his own rash suspicions of the Countess; his love was redoubled; he was impatient to receive her in his arms; and all the lively impressions of delight and satisfaction which he felt were communicated to his friends. Chauvigny embraced him in joyful congratulation; Randolph forgot his suspicions, and wore a face of serenity and pleasure. A generous repast was prepared, and the board was graced with the most enlivened social festivity. The false host knew full well the dreadful purpose now to be executed, and dared not oppose, though he shuddered at the thought of it. To Reginhald he resigned the absolute command of his domestics. The wicked Monk was officiously attentive to oblige Lord Salisbury; eager to promote the joy of the table, but less intent on sharing in this joy, than in providing for the guests. He had now mixed the fatal draught, and saw the poisoned bowl in the hand of an attendant, ready to be delivered to Lord William. He stood unnoticed in a distant part of the hall; his heart panting, his limbs trembling, and his haggard eyes fixed upon the Earl. He saw him receive the bowl; he retired towards the entrance of the hall; he heard him salute his host and his associates; he turned, and saw him raise the poison towards his head.—In that instant he rushed impetuously out, regardless of those who were entering with equal haste; mounted his horse, which stood prepared by his appointment, and, in an extravagance of horrid and malignant joy, fled to Lord Raymond with the important news that the Earl of Salisbury was no more.

The joy of Raymond was wild and extravagant. With eyes all on fire, and accents faltering with impatience and emotion, he demanded the particulars of this surprising intelligence; and the shameless and abandoned wickedness of Reginhald scrupled not to declare the whole of his adventures since his late departure from the castle. He was heard with eagerness and anxiety. At the mention of poison Raymond trembled; the blood forsook his cheeks, and his brow bespoke horror and consternation: but Grey laboured to quiet his disordered spirit, by observing, that he had taken no part in the deed; that it was past and irrevocable; that, now, he had but to consider how to improve this event to his own advantage, to the interests of his love and fortune. The wretch who hath once deviated from the paths of goodness, is easily reconciled to the horrors of his progress in iniquity. The thoughts of this Lord were soon turned to the flattering prospects of happiness which were presented to his imagination: his first emotions of joy and triumph returned; he commended the zeal and daring spirit of Reginhald; and Grey joined in the applause, although his wicked heart secretly repined at the share which his brother might now boast, in advancing the designs of Lord Raymond; and envied the vast rewards which his services might justly claim.

Raymond was now fully persuaded that all his wishes were speedily to be crowned with success; that future difficulties would gradually vanish. In his present state of exultation he forgot the obstinacy with which the Countess had hitherto opposed his desires, and flattered himself with the hopes that a little time, together with a full and clear assurance of the death of Salisbury, would prevail on her to listen more favourably to his suit. For a while he resolved to suspend his solicitations; but, as the prospect of success served to inflame his passion, he obstinately adhered to his resolution of possessing this proud Lady, and even of recurring once more to violence, if violence should be necessary. With an affected lenity and generosity he ordered the three followers of William to be dismissed, when he had first severely reproved them, for presuming to disturb the minds of his friends by false intelligence. They returned towards the house of Randolph, still wondering at the delay of their Lord, and impatient to acquaint him with those important tidings, which the unhappy Oswald had found means of giving them in their confinement, notwithstanding the vigilance of their guards.

Nor did these late extraordinary events, which had engaged all the attention of Raymond and his creatures, fail to excite the wonder and expectation of the Countess. They had suspended her persecution, and now gave her leisure to indulge her hopes of relief and deliverance. Such hopes she had not yet resigned, though tormented with delay and painful disappointment. Some fears indeed sometimes arose, to cloud the pleasing thoughts she was studious to entertain: yet when she reflected how abruptly Raymond had retreated from his wicked purpose of forcibly possessing himself of her bed, under the pretence of a nuptial ceremony; when she considered the appearances of commotion and disorder which were evidently discoverable in the castle; she seemed to have good reasons to persuade herself, that some intelligence must have been received, equally favourable to her, and confounding to her oppressor. She expected every moment to hear of the vigorous and effectual interposition of some friends to assert her just rights, and to redeem her from her present captivity; yet did she frequently lament to her faithful attendant, that her rescue was so long delayed. Whatever consolation Elinor could give, was now dissembled and constrained; for Oswald had been enabled to convey to his sister the seizing of young William, and his own return and confinement. She was but too well acquainted with the violence of Ela, too much alarmed with the dread of her relapsing into her former malady, to entrust this fatal intelligence to her ear. With a heart oppressed with grief and terror, she assumed the aspect of ease and serenity. When the Countess expressed her fears, a sigh sometimes escaped from the attendant; but it seemed the sigh of friendly sympathy: and, in her moments of pleasing thoughts and expectations, Elinor had ever at command some general expressions of comfort, some effusions of pious confidence in the great protector of innocence, to brighten the dawn of hope which arose within her gentle mistress. But she was soon to be undeceived; too soon was her heart to be pierced with the most dreadful tidings.

Book VI

SECTION I

The two brothers, who had proved such zealous agents in oppression and cruelty, were once again to aggravate the distresses of the Countess. The discontent and envy which Grey had conceived towards Reginhald since his last arrival, and which he was not studious to conceal, together with the insolence and presumption of this Monk, founded on the opinion of his great services, produced mutual coldness and contempt in their wicked hearts, and threatened to dissolve their iniquitous union. A new and unexpected incident now served to light up their animosity.

Some enormities of Reginhald had lately been discovered in the monastery, too great to be concealed or palliated. A country maiden had been seduced to a compliance with his sensual desires. He had for some time consorted with her, 'till by degrees his brutal passion grew sated, and required some new object. He fixed his lascivious eyes upon the concubine of one of his associates in revelling, and made some attempts to possess her; which had provoked her paramour to utter the most violent menaces against the Monk. To appease his resentment, Reginhald basely proposed to give him up the unhappy victim of his own lewdness. The man was not yet so abandoned to all sense of virtue, as not to feel the utmost abhorrence at this instance of transcendent villainy. Less scrupulous to acknowledge his own shame, as he was not of the clerical order, and too violently provoked against the Monk to admit any thought of reconciliation, he only waited to procure such proofs as might confirm his information; then seized the moment of Reginhald's absence, produced the wretched woman he had corrupted, as well as her he had attempted, and wounded the ears of the reverend fraternity with a full detection of their wicked brother: the whole cloister was instantly filled with sorrow and indignation. Every instance of outrage and irreverence which he had committed was now recalled to mind, and repeated by every tongue. How often he had disturbed or disgraced their religious house, was now freely told; how often his inoffensive brethren had been exposed to his insolence or malice; how often his beastly revels had been prolonged, 'till, roused by the mattin-bell, he had mixed his debauchery with their early devotions. It was at length resolved to send a deputation to the castle of Salisbury to demand that Reginhald should be sent back to his monastery, there to hear his accusers, and to suffer the punishment due to his accumulated baseness.

The persons entrusted with this commission were now arrived. The Monk was made acquainted with the purpose of their coming, and affected to treat them with defiance and contempt, although he was too conscious of his guilt not to feel the most violent secret emotions of terror. He sought his brother, and demanded his advice and assistance in this emergency. They chose for their private conference a garden belonging to the castle, in which the Countess had chiefly delighted in her happier days, and which she now sometimes visited, to refresh her harassed mind. Grey listened to the story of his brother's danger, with a provoking coldness and insensibility. Reginhald rudely vaunted his important services to Hubert and Raymond, and seemed to expect, as his just right, their full protection in this his present difficulty. Grey at length broke silence by lamenting this fatal discovery, which he industriously represented as in the highest degree dangerous and terrible. The Monk could scarcely restrain his impatience, at the affected air of superiority which his brother assumed, and the insolence of reproof and censure which his words conveyed. Grey, as if still desirous to mortify him to the utmost, continued his discourse by observing with what zeal he had laboured to recommend a man to the notice of Lord Raymond, who, he feared, must now appear, in the general eye, as unworthy of the favour of this Lord, and that he himself must share in his disgrace.—"Dog!" exclaimed the Monk, flying furiously upon his brother, who was alarmed, and retired from his violence, which he endeavoured to allay, by hastily promising his friendly interposition with Lord Raymond.—"Thy interposition!" cried Reginhald; "Am I to depend on thee, thou caitiff? Is this my reward? Am I to sue to thee for the protection of thy great friends? Who was it that saved them and their pernicious minion from disgrace and ruin? Thou, indeed, couldst steal away from sanctuary the infant heir of Salisbury: but this was the daring hand which presented the fatal draught to the father."—Here a loud and piercing shriek broke off their discourse. Ela and her kind attendant had taken their seat, unnoticed, in an adjoining bower, and heard the last passionate exclamations of the Monk. The emotion of the Countess was too great to be suppressed. The brothers started, were confounded, and hastily separated; whilst Elinor fled with frantic speed to summon assistance to her mistress.

She was soon conveyed to her chamber, and laid upon her couch, languid and silent. Elinor hung over her with streaming eyes, and ever and anon entreated her to give vent to her sorrows; but they were too great for utterance. Her eyes indeed were sometimes raised to heaven with all the expression of silent misery, and then, again, gently closed, as if inviting the kind and healing hand of death to cover them in eternal darkness. But no complaints did she breathe, no exclamations of anguish did she utter. At length her frame seemed convulsed, and violently agitated: a torrent of tears poured down her lovely cheeks, and Elinor conceived some hopes that her great soul was now struggling to shake off the intolerable weight of sorrow. But the calm which succeeded was the calm of insensibility: she gazed round her with a vacant eye, and all her nobleness of nature seemed irrecoverably lost in senseless melancholy.

The disorder of her deportment had reached the ears of Raymond, and, in the violence of surprise and anxiety, he once again rushed into her presence.—With all the bitterness of remorse, he viewed the majestic ruins of exalted beauty and greatness, the fatal effect of his lawless passions. His haughty soul melted into pity: he demanded the cause of her disorder, and received from Elinor a distinct account of the horrid discourse to which her unhappy Lady had been witness. All the train of dreadful passions that attend on detected guilt, tore the heart of Raymond with their united tortures. He started, and wildly traversed the chamber: he paused; bent his eyes again upon the Countess; then, turning suddenly from the afflicting object, uttered terrible execrations upon himself and his vile seducers. He fell upon his knees, and, addressing himself to Ela, as if she were sensible of his discourse, he passionately vowed to restore her son to her arms, and instantly to abandon her castle.—Again, rising suddenly, and issuing forth with wild precipitation, he called loudly for Grey; who appeared before him trembling, and, to prevent his rage, began with cursing the brutal violence of Reginhald.—"Bid my Knights prepare," said Raymond; "let my retinue stand ready before the gates:—we must depart."—The countenance of his creature expressed surprise and dissatisfaction.—"No expostulation! none of thy damned arts!—Where hast thou bestowed the son of this unhappy woman? See that he be instantly conveyed back to her castle. Do it, slave, or woe upon thy head! Haste!—answer me not.—Give out my orders for departure."—Then, once more entering the chamber of the Countess, with all the remorse and anguish of a man at length awakened to a sense of his unjust misguided conduct, when it was now too late to be corrected or repaired; he gazed distractedly upon her, and with a deep and dismal groan pronounced a solemn farewell. Then turning quickly upon Elinor, who wept by his side: "Speak to her," said he; "she disdains, and justly, to hold converse with a villain. Say, that her persecution is now ended. Tell her I knew not, I contrived not the murder of her husband. Let her pronounce his doom, and the officious slave that acted the foul deed shall die. Her son lives, and shall yet be happy in her embraces.—Hear me, woman! Tell her I am gone: gone, nevermore to torment the weak, unfriended, solitary widow.—Yes! those cheeks are yet lovely; that form still noble. But what of that? For me! for me could heaven have reserved so rich a treasure? Horrid presumption!"—Elinor kneeled before him, petitioned with all humility for the enlargement of her brother, and that, to assist her in the necessary attendance on the unhappy Countess, he might be ordered to reside for some time in the castle.—"Cursed castle," cried Raymond; "cursed be the hour in which I first entered these fatal walls! And forever cursed be the slaves who forced me, against my better reason, to persevere in cruelty."—

In the midst of this frenzy, he was surprised into some degree of composure, by the appearance of a stranger, who, forcing his way violently into the apartment, approached towards the Countess, with an air and aspect of affection and reverence. He accosted her, without deigning to cast a look upon Lord Raymond; and soon perceived the wretched state to which she was reduced. "What!" cried he, "no ear for joy and comfort! no voice to greet the arrival of an old faithful servant!"—Raymond, advancing with a stern and haughty frown, demanded to know who he was, and what the cause of this bold unmannered intrusion. "Question thy own base hinds," said he, "who dared to forbid my approach.—Nay, let thy weapon rest; I have a sword as keen, and an arm as brave as thine."—Raymond here attempted to summon his attendants.—"Beware, proud Lord," continued the stranger; "poor as I am, single as I am in the midst of thy creatures, I fear not the power of Lord Raymond. The least violence done to this person would be instantly repaid with ten-fold vengeance. If this noble dame hath been reduced to her present state of misery by thee—hear, and tremble. Thy usurped authority is expired: I am the harbinger of Earl William. Yes! thou hast cause to tremble: my Lord, my gracious master, the princely Salisbury, approaches, and, before the close of day, shall resume his rightful power and authority within these walls."—Here, Elinor, who had listened in amazement, fell suddenly on her knees, returned thanks to heaven with the most rapturous devotion, and called passionately upon her mistress to hear the joyful tidings; but was answered only by a deep and heart-felt sigh.

The soul of Raymond was harrowed with consternation. He stood speechless and motionless, and suffered the stranger to depart without farther question. He found himself on the brow of a fatal precipice, whither he had been fatally misled by the wickedness of his flatterers, and now was prevented from retreating. Justice followed close upon him, and vengeance was ready to push him head-long down. After an hideous pause of dismay, he rushed out, and once more called furiously for Grey: but Grey had heard the fatal intelligence, and hid himself from the fury of his Lord, which echoed loudly through the halls. The attendants were collected round him, whom he ordered instantly to prepare for their departure, and to retire from this accursed place. He loudly and frequently called out, "To horse!" still ranging madly through the castle in search of Grey. In this state of distraction he chanced to espy the Monk, who trembled and shrunk from him, in abject terror. "Traitor!" cried Raymond, seizing him by the throat, "thy falsehood hath done this. Thou hast listened to mine enemies, and been their agent to abuse me by thy falsehoods, to deceive and destroy me: but thou at least shalt feel my vengeance." Reginhald fell at his feet, and would have expostulated; but the storm in the breast of Raymond was too violent to be allayed by his submissions. The unhappy Lord, fully persuaded that the Monk had purposedly framed a tale to lull him into false security, called to his followers, and commanded them to hang up the traitor. "There," said he, sternly repeating his command, and pointing to a large oak which stood in view, near the castle walls; "there let me see my sentence executed without delay." And without delay did they proceed to execute this dreadful sentence. The wicked Reginhald, condemned by the man for whom he had proceeded to such enormous guilt, was led away, in vain imploring mercy, urging the unmerited severity of his fate, and gnashing his teeth in rage and despair. Grey, from his place of concealment, was terrified with the view of his brother in the agonies of death, and tortured with the fear of becoming the next victim to the distracted violence of Raymond.

SECTION II

The dreadful intelligence, now received, was speedily and fatally confirmed to these wicked intruders. Heaven had graciously watched over the Earl of Salisbury, and, with a wonderful hand, rescued him from the brink of destruction. Just in that moment when the cup, poisoned by the Monk, had reached and wet his lips, a sudden exclamation from Chauvigny surprised and discomposed him. He started and withdrew the fatal draught. The noise was loud in the hall, and the crowd increased: his eyes quickly encountered Les Roches rushing eagerly forward: the cup fell from his hand, and he pressed on with equal ardour to meet the embraces of his long-lost friend. They clung together in that tumult of joy which knows no words: and, when at length Les Roches found leisure to turn to Chauvigny, the gentle youth, pressing him earnestly in his arms, completed his happiness, by exclaiming, that Jacqueline too was safe. Nature was exhausted by these violent emotions, and Les Roches sunk down upon a seat, breathless and silent. Again recovering, he cast his eyes round, and surveyed the well-known countenances of his followers and associates, the attendants of Chauvigny, and some of the brave soldiers of Lord William. He started up, and pressed the hands of each: then again, turning to his two noble friends, again he gazed upon them with eager joy, and again they renewed their embraces. "Now," said the Earl, "I shall indeed return home in triumph: now are all my toils, my terrors and dangers, amply recompensed." Then, resuming his seat at the table, he invited Les Roches to share in their repast, and to allow some indulgence and refreshment to his fatigue.—"And hast thou, indeed, preserved my daughter?" cried the Frenchman. "Let me see her! let her father take the dear treasure to his arms!

Is she well? Is she at hand?"—"Safely bestowed under the hospitable roof of this good Knight," replied William, and pointed to Randolph. "The noble maid shall straight be summoned to meet thee, and soon shall she share thy joy."—"Thanks to the eternal goodness!" replied Les Roches, "that goodness which hath been pleased to unite us to each other by mutual and repeated offices of friendship. Lo! for my daughter, I present thee with a gift as precious." Then beckoning to one of his followers, who had entered with him, the man retired, and soon returned, leading young William in his hand, who flew to his father with tears of infant joy. The astonishment of the Earl could scarcely allow him leisure to return the fond endearments of his son. He looked wildly on his friend, and seemed to demand an explanation of this wonder. "Yes," said Les Roches, "thou dost embrace thy son, rescued from danger, perhaps from destruction.—But be calm. Thou shalt be satisfied. Hear then the story of my fortunes, since I was last separated from thee, my dearest Chauvigny. A few words will relate it all.

"Thou hast already heard (Lord William) how much I am indebted to this noble youth. He hath informed thee, no doubt, of our preparations for seeking thee in England, and of our adventure with the pirate who attempted to seize our vessel; little suspecting that strength and desperate resolution which soon taught him to consult his safety by a precipitate flight. Just in that instant when the swelling waters had separated our ships, and our enemies were crowding their sails to escape from that force which they had rashly provoked, their captain had been borne down by the press, and lay at the feet of one of our brave followers, whose sword was now ready to descend with fury upon his head. But I stopped his arm; and, perceiving our situation, that we were unseconded, and now surrounded by our enemies, I deemed it madness to provoke them by any farther resistance. I yielded myself a prisoner; and the few who had leaped on board with me, soon followed my example. At first, the attention of our enemies was wholly engaged on securing their escape. When they had left our vessel at sufficient distance, their captain accosted me; and, with a gloomy courtesy, thanked me for rescuing him from his danger. I answered, that, as he had experienced our valour, and, when we still might have sold our liberties at a dearer rate, we had declined the effusion of blood, I hoped he would treat us nobly. He demanded to know who we were, and what our purpose. He had taken us, he said, for merchants; that, as he approached, our numbers and appearance had alarmed his people; but, as we had made every attempt in our power to avoid him, he was encouraged to persevere in his design of attacking us: that he himself lived by plunder, and he suspected, that we were engaged in the same pursuit.—If so, we might unite our force with his, and share his fortunes. To convince him of his mistake, I informed him freely of my country, my condition, and my destination, earnestly conjuring him to restore me to my companions, and promising the most ample rewards for a service so important. 'Let me but once regain my countrymen,' said I, 'and they shall enrich thee with such a ransom, as shall exceed thy wishes.' But not all my promises could prevail upon the pirate again to seek our ship. He had experienced our force, and dreaded a severe revenge for his attempt. Yet my repeated solicitations at length so far prevailed, that, after some time ineffectually roving in search of prey, he proposed to keep three of my companions and myself on board, to land the rest, with a small number of his own men, on the coast of England, (as it was probable our friends had sought this coast) and that, if they could regain them, and send back the stipulated ransom, I should then be free. I gladly embraced this proposal. The pirate steered towards the land: the coast was alarmed at the sight of his vessel: but, to prevent all opposition, we chose the dead hour of night, and sent off our men in a boat, which brought them unnoticed to shore. They travelled for some time, e're they had the good fortune to find those of our attendants whom Lord Chauvigny had left to treat for my liberty. At length, however, they were found; and the men returned, unmolested, with my ransom. To this I added a rich jewel taken from my finger, which I presented to the pirate, in acknowledgement of my gratitude.

"I now hastened to join my friends, and from them I learned that Lord Chauvigny had proceeded to the city of Marlborough. I was earnest to follow him, but my fatigues demanded some refreshment. I was conducted to the house of an inhabitant of the coast, who received me with all hospitable kindness.—Let us unite in adoring the invisible power that directed my steps thither!—The friendly repast was prepared for me; nor were my followers neglected. I was pleased at the honest undesigning affection of my host, and taught to revere the generous people amongst whom fortune had now placed me. At the hour of rest, I was courteously conducted to my chamber, but my mind had been too long and too violently agitated to admit repose. I revolved the dangers and distresses I had experienced: I thought of the great purpose for which I had visited this country: I thought of my daughter and my friend: I sometimes indulged my hopes of finding them, and, again, checked and condemned these flattering imaginations. Thus did I pass the weary night, 'till, roused by a voice in the adjacent chamber, I listened attentively, and heard my host in earnest conference with his wife. 'I like not,' said he, 'this message from the castle of Salisbury.'—I started at the name, and redoubled my attention.—'This boy is to be carefully guarded and concealed. But, wherefore? Lord Raymond is to wed the widow of the Earl. Why then this concealment, unless he purposes to destroy the young heir? I know the soul of Grey; and, though he be my brother, our souls are not allied. I dread his temper. Nature formed him stern and cruel; nor do I doubt but that he may easily be wrought upon to act a deed of blood. But shall my humble dwelling be made the scene of murder, of an infant's murder?'—His wife here began to chide his jealous fears; but they seemed to have taken too deep root in his mind to be easily removed. 'What, though my house should not be made the place of execution?' said this good man; 'What, though they should not proceed to the utmost pitch of cruelty? Their purpose cannot be honest, and I am made their accomplice by concealing him.'—I had heard enough; and now I busily revolved this alarming discourse: It was evident that the son of my preserver was exposed to danger—perhaps abandoned by his widow—(pardon me, Lord William, if my suspicion was rash and ungentle)—certainly concealed for some mysterious purpose. A stranger seemed to pity, and to fear for him; What then became a friend? What was the part of Les Roches? Were his father still alive, Heaven had now enabled me to restore him to his arms: but, if he really hath perished, surely it must be my care to protect and cherish this boy, to form the unhappy orphan to honour and virtue, to make him worthy of his illustrious descent, and enable him, in due time, to assert his native rights.—Thus I reasoned; and, rising with the early dawn, summoned my followers, communicated this important discovery, and desired their counsel and assistance. They readily concurred in the design of rescuing the young Lord from his present danger. By their advice I waited the appearance of our host. I accosted him gently, and led him on to discourse of his situation, his condition, his friends and his country. He answered me without reserve, 'till I at length mentioned the name of Earl William, and asked if he could inform me of the fortunes of this Lord, and his noble house. He started, and answered, hesitating and confused. I at once sternly told him, I was no stranger to the designs formed against the young heir of that house: that, as I had been a friend to the father, I resolved to be a protector to the son, who, I knew, was concealed under this roof. If he would consent to give him up peaceably into my hands, the service should be duly rewarded; if not—I had force sufficient to rescue him from danger. The man trembled, and, without delay, resigned his charge into my hands.—And now was my mind possessed with new fears and scruples. Methought I had been too rash. A mother's tenderness, perhaps, hath concealed this boy, and, for a weighty cause, no doubt. How then shall the news of this violent removal afflict her soul? What terrors must she feel? Yet, still, upon mature reflection, I deemed it the safest course to convey this youth to Marlborough, where I hoped to gain such intelligence as might direct my future conduct. Thither we bent our course; and, near this place, did I receive those joyful tidings, which brought me to deliver up my dear charge into his father's care."

"From my soul I thank thee," replied the Earl.—"Yet hath thy tale renewed some doubts and suspicions—but let suspicions sleep till to-morrow." Then, starting up earnestly, he asked with a loud voice, "Who of my brave followers will undertake the charge of repairing instantly to Cornwall, bearing to the fair Jacqueline the cheering news of her father's arrival, and conveying her to my castle?" Fitz-Alan stood forth, and, with five more who defied toil and fatigue, insisted that this pleasing charge should be entrusted to them. They departed, fresh and vigorous as the sturdy hind that rises to his morning labours. And now Lord William, turning kindly towards Les Roches, attempted once more to speak his joy and gratitude. But suddenly his voice failed, his cheeks grew pale, a cold dew issued from his pores, his whole frame was disordered, and he sunk faintly down. The guests arose in confusion and amazement. Tyrrel trembled in an agony of terror, nor was his consternation unobserved.—"Treason," cried Chauvigny, seizing the false host, "and this sword shall revenge it.—But what revenge on thee, thou wretched slave?— Say, Hast thou indeed murdered this noble Lord? Hath thy vile hand dealt him poison? Confess thy villainy, or this moment is thy last." The abject Tyrrel had fallen on his knees, and now loudly and vehemently asserted his innocence; but, when terrified by the view of instant death, he scrupled not to confess, that, by the direction of Lord Hubert, he had invited the Earl to his house, but that he was not privy to any deadly purpose; if such had been concerted, the Monk alone was privy, the Monk alone had executed it. Reginhald was sought for, but he had fled, which confirmed their suspicions, and filled the hall with grief and dismay. William alone seemed unmoved. He gently pressed the hand of Les Roches: "My enemies have prevailed," said he, "the snares of Hubert have caught me.—Alas! thou knowest him not.—Visit my castle, comfort my wife, and Oh! continue thy kind protection to my son."

The grief of Lord Chauvigny was outrageous: that of Les Roches had choked his voice. He hung over the languid Earl, in silence and consternation; whilst, on the other hand, the boy clung passionately round the knees of his father. The scene was affecting; and even the rough soldier, to whom death had been long familiar, melted into tears.—"Poisoned! and by Lord Hubert!" was repeated with sorrow and indignation. The dismal tidings were soon caught by busy tongues, spread abroad, and propagated through the land, to aggravate the disgrace the wicked favourite was soon to experience.

His afflicted friends conveyed the Earl to his couch. And, now, the good old Randolph, whose venerable face had worn the deepest marks of sorrow, seemed to be suddenly enlivened by a gleam of hope. He paused, appeared earnest to collect his dissipated thoughts, and now looked, as a man unexpectedly visited by comfort. The eyes of his friends were fixed upon him, as if demanding an explanation; when, addressing himself hastily to Lord William, he asked of his present state, whether his pain was increased, or his languor more oppressing? He thanked the gentle Knight, and declared, that now he seemed more at ease.—"Yes," cried Randolph, "and soon shall this malady cease, and still shall William live."—The Frenchmen were astonished, but the Knight confidently repeated his joyful assurances. Experienced and sagacious, and accustomed to survey all objects with more calmness and composure than young Chauvigny, he revolved all the incidents, since their arrival at the house of Tyrrel. He had marked the aspect of the Monk, and from thence had formed the blackest suspicions of his temper and designs. He had marked his officious cares, and obsequious zeal in attending on the Earl. He had marked how, at the first entrance of Les Roches, the cup had dropped from the hands of Salisbury. He recollected, that after this the Monk had not been seen; and justly concluded, that this was the fatal cup which had been prepared for his friend; that the fell purpose of Hubert had been happily defeated by his sudden surprise; and that the poisonous mixture, which, if drank, must have instantly proved fatal, had now, when but just scarcely tasted, raised a temporary disorder in the frame of William, which nature, still free from deep infection, would soon be able to overcome. These thoughts, which he communicated to his noble companions, were received with joy; and soon were they confirmed by that ease and vigour which the Earl gradually recovered. Tyrrel had been secured, and was now examined at more leisure. His discoveries served to convince them of what was really the truth, that he had indeed connived at the base design, but not been directly an assistant. But he was not an object worthy of noble revenge. Against Lord Hubert was vengeance loudly denounced, and the great soul of Salisbury was on fire to inflict the full severity of justice on his treachery and unrelenting malice.

His resentment and indignation were still to be more inflamed. The unhappy Oswald, who had for some time groaned under a severe captivity, at length had found means to make some impression on the heart of his keeper, who kindly consented to relax his hardships. When the messengers of Lord William were confined, he had desired, and was secretly admitted to hold some conference with them. The keeper was witness, with what clearness and ingenuous honesty they entered into the detail of all their fortunes, and declared that their Lord must, e're long, appear to confront his enemies. The man was alarmed: he had heard the story of Oswald, and he heard it now repeated with honest pity and indignation. He was persuaded, that the power of Lord Raymond was soon to expire; and that he should do an acceptable service to the Earl, by favouring the escape of that man who had been punished for his affection to the Countess. He revolved these thoughts for some time; at length listened to the solicitations of his prisoners, and suffered Oswald to escape. He lay concealed for a while, resolving to take his way cautiously towards Cornwall; but soon learned the important tidings, which, by this time, began to spread through the adjacent country, that the Earl of Salisbury had arrived at Marlborough, and was preparing to return to his castle. He therefore changed his course, and directed his wary steps towards the royal seat. Fortunately, he encountered Fitz-Alan and his companions, who informed him where he might find their noble master. He entered the hall of Tyrrel at midnight, and demanded to be instantly conducted to the Earl. Alarmed at that general sorrow and dismay which dwelt upon every face, he ventured to enquire, and was soon informed of the cause.—"Alas!" said he, "if the malice of his enemies hath reached the Earl, how shall Oswald hope to escape?" Then, sitting down in mournful silence, he passed the heavy hours in all the bitterness of anguish and despair, 'till the dawn of morning.

The friends and vassals of the Earl, who by this time began to collect round their Lord, had scarcely felt the alarm of his danger, when they received the joyful tidings of his recovery. Oswald too was cheered, and again demanded immediate admittance to the Earl. And he was soon admitted, for his appearance and demeanour promised something extraordinary. He kneeled before Lord William, and wept.—"I come," said he, "from thy castle. I come to tell thee of thy unhappy Countess."—The agitation of the Earl grew violent: but he commanded him to proceed, and he heard him with breathless attention; 'till Oswald, who began to relate all the events of the castle of Salisbury, which he had known, proceeded without reserve to describe the oppression of Lord Raymond, with an artless and ingenuous freedom. The rage of William was kindled: he started wildly from his seat, and thundered out the most terrible denunciations of vengeance and destruction.—"So may this arm prosper. So may this good sword do me service in the hour of danger, as I will revenge thee, noble dame! And may I be cursed, and scorned, and vile as thee, thou recreant Lord, if I forget thy treachery and oppression.—But come, my friends! let us away!—O murderous thief! Is it thus thy wolfish nature hath stolen in upon my helpless fold!"—His friends laboured to recall him to calmness and attention. Oswald proceeded in his tale, and filled the breasts of all his hearers with the most enlivened indignation. He concluded with relating the reception of the messengers, and his own escape, humbly imploring the protection of the Earl against his incensed Lord. "May heaven forget me," replied William, "if I forget thy honesty. But come, my friends! if ever pity softened your breasts, if ever manhood dwelt in your noble hearts, assist me in punishing the injuries of my gentle Countess."—Here young William entered, and ran fondly to embrace his father. At sight of him Oswald fell upon his knees, and, with an extravagance of pious joy, thanked the gracious powers who had preserved him. The boy turned and acknowledged his former protector. Thus was the truth of all that Oswald had delivered wonderfully confirmed; and William renewed his thanks and promises of favour. The attendants were summoned: every moment brought in more and more of the Earl's vassals: Les Roches, Chauvigny, and Randolph vied with each other in their expressions of zeal and impatience to redress the injured. All were ready to take their way, and William enjoyed the pleasing thoughts of surprising the base usurpers in the midst of their presumption. But Fitz-Alan had prevented this surprise. He could not suppress his impatient affection for his noble mistress. To delight her with the first joyful tidings of her Lord's approach, he had turned aside and visited the castle; and there did he raise that confusion which had overwhelmed Lord Raymond, and his wicked creature.

SECTION III

But whilst the anguish and consternation of Raymond, which arose from shame and remorse, grew every moment more violent; Grey, who was concerned solely for his personal safety, gradually regained some share of recollection, and began to consider of the means to ward off the impending danger from his own head. His chief reliance was on the important service which he conceived to be in his own power, that of discovering the residence of young William, and restoring him to his father. But still farther to increase his merit, and to atone for past offences, he determined to betray his master, and to give him up, naked and defenceless, into the hands of his enemies. This base resolution once formed, no time was to be lost in executing it: Raymond was preparing to depart; this must be instantly prevented. He flew among his followers and attendants: he represented the danger which now threatened them, in the most alarming colours: he told them, that their Lord had long proceeded in a course of injustice and oppression, which must be now revenged with indiscriminate fury on all who had accompanied him: that he now prepared to retire, hoping, that, whilst the injured Earl was taking a bloody vengeance on his innocent followers, he might escape in the confusion: that the only means of providing for their safety, of approving their innocence, and of disarming the resentment of Lord William, was to continue in their present situation, without any appearance of hostile intentions, any purpose of opposing the entrance of the rightful Lord of this castle, and to oblige their leader also to stay and answer for his own actions. To the nobler few he hinted these things with caution, and they received his insinuations with disdain, loudly declaring that they were resolved to live or die with

Raymond. To the baser and the greater number he spoke more plainly. To them he scrupled not to declare, that the violent passions of their Lord had disordered his understanding, and asked, with well-affected terror, who could be safe, after the outrageous dealing with his unhappy brother, whose only fault was, that he had served Lord Raymond (alas!) with too blind and too violent a zeal.—They heard him with approbation, and readily consented to submit to his direction, in this dangerous emergency.

The unhappy Raymond was now reduced to the lowest state of human wretchedness; tormented with the consciousness of his own guilt and weakness; unable to repair, or to atone for, the mischief he had occasioned; pierced with all the stings of remorse; unable to conceal his disgrace, yet still too great of soul to bear it: helpless and solitary, whilst the arm of vengeance was lifted against him; deserted by his followers, and betrayed by the man whose wicked arts had sunk him into this depth of misery. Grey, on the other hand, seemed to have composed his fears, and to enjoy a short-lived triumph. He had collected a party round him, which gave him the command of the castle. His Lord had retired to give his distractions some moments of rest; and his creature now issued out orders to his associates, to watch his motions, and even to oppose his departure by force.

In the midst of his presumption, he sought Lord Raymond, whom he had but now avoided with the most abject terror: with an insolent composure he desired him to explain his intentions.—"Oh! are you come?" cried Raymond:—"I have commanded my people to prepare for departure. Let us this instant be gone!"—"Whither?" said Grey. "How shall we escape? Whither shall we fly? The powers of Earl William are at hand.—But what of that? His resentment is not directed against us. We have not sought to pollute his bed. We have not destroyed the repose and happiness of his wife."—His Lord started up in sudden fury, as if preparing to punish this insolence: but Grey, nothing dismayed, bade him compose his passions: they had already proved too violent.—"Alas!" said he, "What was the crime of my unhappy brother?—Guilty indeed he was, but not to thee, cruel Lord. But I will not upbraid thee now.—Those followers, whom Raymond cannot protect, he must no longer hope to command.—Nay, my Lord, seek not to pass: here thou hast no longer power; this chamber must content thee: here must Earl William find thee. Answer him as thou mayest."—There only wanted this treacherous insolence, to fill up the mighty sum of miseries, under which Raymond groaned. He found himself indeed a prisoner, guarded by his own people, and in the absolute power of his perfidious creature. He stood in mute surprise; and Grey was just preparing to repeat his insolence, when the noise of horsemen called him suddenly forth.

A small troop had been descried at a considerable distance, pressing forward towards the castle, with the most violent and precipitate speed. Those of Raymond's attendants, who had refused to unite in the treachery of Grey, first espied their approach, and, mounting their horses, called for their Lord to stand on his defence, or bravely to lead them against the enemy (for such they deemed them.) But Grey now appeared, and, with a sudden recollection of thought, told them, in the name of Raymond, that no resistance was to be attempted: that their Lord feared not, nor would oppose these visitors: but that he directed his friends to march a mile eastward of the castle, and there to expect him. They obeyed; and Grey now observed the little troop more distinctly, wondering at the small number, and struck with a sudden and instinctive terror, when he discovered Lord William (whose person he well knew) at the head of this company. He gazed earnestly round him, yet, still, but a few persons only were in view.—"By heavens!" cried Grey, "he comes not with a force to drive us hence, but to make himself our prisoner:" then hastily ordered his associates to suffer these men to enter unopposed and unmolested, and, instantly afterwards, to shut fast the castle-gates. He cursed his own folly and rashness, which had led him to betray himself to Lord Raymond. He now saw a noble occasion of repairing his fault, and, instead of persevering in his resolution of giving up Raymond into the hands of the Earl, he now deemed it in his power, and judged it the wisest course to give up the Earl into the hands of his Lord.

SECTION IV

William had indeed exposed himself to the utmost danger, by his ungoverned violence. He had taken his way at the head of a princely retinue, well appointed, and zealous to vindicate his cause; so that now his port was that of a warlike Baron, marching to assist his King, against some sudden invasion. Part of his powers was directed to advance towards the castle by different approaches, so as to surround it, and prevent the escape of Raymond or his people. He himself, at the head of a chosen band, attended by the two French nobles, rushed directly forward. But the impetuosity of the Earl soon left his attendants at a distance, all but young Chauvigny and a few others, who with difficulty kept pace with him. They arrived at the castle-gates, without perceiving that they were come unsupported; and William, far from recollecting his danger, rushed on with furious and impatient ardour, 'till he had reached the apartment of the Countess.

He flew to take her in his arms, and started back in an agony of terror and surprise, at the discovery of her unhappy condition. He called upon her with earnest, yet tender accents; and now nature seemed to make some efforts to shake off its lethargic weight. The Countess trembled, as at some extraordinary appearance; gazed with a look less vacant, as if the dawn of reason were returning; sighed and wept.—"Art thou," said the Earl, turning to Elinor, who busily assisted him to support her mistress, "Art thou that good matron, whose cares have administered comfort to my wife?—Heaven shall reward thee; and William shall not be unmindful of thy honest affection. But say—conceal not the truth:—Whence this sad disorder in her noble mind? Hath not her oppressor completed his vile design? Hath he not forcibly taken possession of her bed?"—Elinor assured him, that heaven had been pleased to preserve her from such pollution; but that, surprised by the shocking tidings of his death, she had lately fallen into this her present state of melancholy.—William again pressed the hand of Ela. "Speak to me," cried he; "say that thou rejoicest at my return.—No word of congratulation! No look of joy! Is this the happiness which my busy fancy formed? Is this my reception?"—The Countess gazed upon him, and seemed in violent agitation: but still she was unable to return his affection. Reason had not yet regained its seat.—At length, the Earl, whose heart was torn with anguish, bounded furiously from the ground where he had fixed his knee, and, loudly demanding the vile murderer of his peace, issued forth in search of Raymond.

By this time the castle was in confusion. Chauvigny and his few attendants had been prevented, by superior numbers, from following Earl William. They expressed their surprise, and now began too late to perceive their danger. One of them, suddenly taking a horn from his side, prepared to give so shrill a blast, as would have reached the ears of their companions, and quickened their speed: but Grey, who now had the sole command, as suddenly prevented him, by declaring, with a stern insolence, that the least alarm should prove immediate death to Lord William. His design, which he now sought to execute, was to raise a violent broil and tumult in the castle, and to assassinate the Earl, in the confusion. The presence and interposition of Raymond he deemed necessary; and he hastened to summon this Lord, to embrace the fair occasion of destroying his rival, which fortune presented to him. At first entering the apartment, his eyes were wounded by an object of terror, which at once confounded all his designs. Raymond had fallen upon his sword. Grey started back in amazement; and, in that moment, William entered and saw the unhappy Lord, pale and bleeding on the ground, who shut his languid eyes, as if ashamed to meet the countenance of him he had wronged. The art, the hypocrisy, the boldness and recollection of Grey, all deserted him. He stood trembling and confounded, awed by the presence of the Earl, as by that of a superior being. At length he attempted to retire; but William, drawing his sword, forbade him with a terrible authority, and demanded the meaning of what he now beheld. Raymond, lifting his eyes faintly, just found breath, at broken and painful intervals, to declare, that his own hand had done it.—"I have indeed wronged thee, Lord; nor could I endure thy triumph, and my own shame—Yes, I have destroyed the noblest Lady.—But there stands the accursed wretch, the false and traitorous"—Here his emotion grew too violent for his languid condition. He was seized with a sudden pang; he groaned and expired.

The Earl then, turning to Grey, exclaimed—"Yes! I know thee now! Thou art the wretch who laboured to aggravate the distresses of Ela, with such infernal diligence. Thou art he who basely stole away my son."—Grey fell upon his knees, supplicating for mercy with the most abject and servile fear, and promising to restore young William. The Earl raised his arm, and prepared to strike the miscreant. "Kill me not!" cried Grey, "or thy son is forever lost. I alone know the secret of his present residence."—Here a sudden and violent shout arrested the sword of William. His followers had arrived, had found the gates barred against their entrance, had quickly forced them open, and rushed, in a rapid torrent, through the halls. Les Roches and Chauvigny, Randolph and Oswald, directed by the outcries of Grey, and the loud rage of Salisbury, forced in, just as the wicked agent of oppression was entreating for mercy. At sight of Oswald, despair pierced his foul heart; and, when he espied young William led on and protected from the violence of the rout, he closed his eyes, and crouched to receive the deadly blow.—"O shame to manhood!" cried Randolph, "shall such a slave die by the arm of William? Look there! noble Lord: (pointing from the window to the body of Reginhald, which still hung from the oak) behold! thy just vengeance is prevented. Behold the punishment which befits such vileness!"—"Be it so," cried William, "well dost thou instruct me!"—And, without farther respite, was Grey led forth to share the fate of his wicked brother.

The view of blood and death allayed the joy of William and his noble friends. The good old Knight was moved, and now seemed to regret that the just punishment of Grey had not been inflicted but by absolute and violent power. All the late dismal effects of lawless oppression crowded into his mind; and he felt the want of that inestimable blessing, a wise, righteous, and well attempered rule.

The thoughts of Ela, and her unhappy condition, still diffused a gloom over the countenance of the Earl. His thanks and congratulations were grave and solemn. The body of Raymond was removed; his attendants were suffered to depart unmolested; order and tranquillity were restored in the castle; and Lord William was at leisure to inform his noble friends of that terrible impression, which her misfortunes had made upon his wife. They had scarcely began to offer condolence and comfort, when Elinor appeared with earnest looks, beseeching the Earl instantly to visit her afflicted Lady. The sight of him had awakened her to some degree of reason, and his removal had excited in her mind a violent and dangerous emotion of fear and anxiety. He hastened to her presence, leading his young son, who ran to the arms of his mother. She hung upon the dear objects with tenderness and pleasure, and uttered some words of joy. That melancholy which had clouded her noble mind, began gradually to dissipate. At length she looked, as if roused from a dream of misery; returned the ardent caresses of her husband, and breathed out her pious thanks to that goodness which had preserved him. A little time so far contributed to compose her mind, that she required the story of her husband's fortunes and dangers. But this he suspended, until her health should be confirmed, and her mind less subject to violent emotions.

Jacqueline was now arrived; had embraced her father and her lover, and was presented to the Countess. At sight of her, Ela felt some agitation, and recollected the tidings which Oswald had conveyed to her. But when William informed her, that he had saved and protected this maid from danger; that she was daughter to a dear friend, to whom he owed his life; and betrothed to a noble youth, both of whom were now in the castle; she embraced her with a tender affection, and secretly felt some shame at her former suspicions. And now the two Barons of France and the old Knight were admitted to offer their congratulations to the Countess. The friends of Earl William crowded from different parts to share his joy, and the castle was for some days a scene of gladness and festivity. But Chauvigny, impatient to complete his happiness, gently urged to Les Roches the necessity of returning to France. William was soon acquainted with their purpose. "Not so!" said he. "Shall I not be witness of the happiness now to crown the virtues of that dear maid, the lovely companion of my dangers, and comforter of my distress? Here, even here, shall her plighted hand be given to Lord Chauvigny!"—Les Roches consented: the nuptial rites were prepared, and celebrated with all due solemnity.

The two sons of Randolph had attended Jacqueline to the castle; and now she earnestly entreated their father to permit them to accompany her to France. "They shall be my Knights," said she, "and shall be treated with all honourable care." The Countess requested, with equal earnestness, that Randolph would permit them to live with her son. But the fond father could not yield to these solicitations: he declared that his sons must first endeavour to render themselves more worthy of such favour.

The faithful Elinor still attended on her beloved mistress, and was entertained with an affection which made the remembrance of her former misfortunes less bitter. Her brother too found that respect and reward which his honest zeal had so justly merited.

The resentment of the Earl against Lord Hubert was in some degree disarmed, when he received the tidings, that this wicked favourite had forfeited the royal grace, and was ignominiously banished. He now reflected on his wrongs with less emotion. Ela too seemed to forget her sufferings, and each was the more endeared to the other, by the late dangers and distresses of their separation.

THE END

Acknowledgements

The publisher and editor wish to thank: Jim Rockhill and Ray Russell, for their continued support; Ellen McDermott for the use of her photograph "Never Let Me Go" for the cover; Meggan Kehrli for her design work; and finally, the National Library of Ireland, for providing a copy of the first Irish edition of *Longsword* for consultation.

Longsword, Earl of Salisbury
was published in two volumes by
W. Johnston, Ludgate Street, London (1762).

A single volume Irish edition was published
in the same year by George Faulkner, Dublin.

About the Author

Thomas Leland (1722-1785) was born in Dublin. Ordained to ministry in the Church of Ireland, his works include *History of Philip, King of Macedon* (1758), *History of Ireland* (1773), and a posthumous collection of sermons (1788). His only work of fiction, *Longsword, Earl of Salisbury*, was published in 1762. It was adapted for stage in 1765 as *The Countess of Salisbury* by fellow Dubliner Hall Hartson. The play remained popular into the early nineteenth century.

About the Editor

Albert Power is an established commentator on Irish writers of the macabre from the early 1700s to the mid-nineteenth century. He has written several articles on these writers for *The Green Book*, as well as commemorative essays on J. S. Le Fanu, and, in 2015, he edited and introduced a new edition of Le Fanu's 1848 novella, *Marston of Dunoran*. Albert's own Augustan-Gothic fiction, *Slaver Heap: A Gothic Novel* and *Georgian Gothic: A Novella Quartet*, appeared in 2013 (revised 2016) and 2014 respectively. His novella collection *Azerbaijan Tales* was published by Egaeus Press in 2021.

SWAN RIVER PRESS

Founded in 2003, Swan River Press is an independent publishing company, based in Dublin, Ireland, dedicated to gothic, supernatural, and fantastic literature. We specialise in limited edition hardbacks, publishing fiction from around the world with an emphasis on Ireland's contributions to the genre.

www.swanriverpress.ie

"Handsome, beautifully made volumes . . . altogether irresistible."

– Michael Dirda, *Washington Post*

"It [is] often down to small, independent, specialist presses to keep the candle of horror fiction flickering . . . "

– Darryl Jones, *Irish Times*

"Swan River Press has emerged as one of the most inspiring new presses over the past decade. Not only are the books beautifully presented and professionally produced, but they aspire consistently to high literary quality and originality, ranging from current writers of supernatural/weird fiction to rare or forgotten works by departed authors."

– Peter Bell, *Ghosts & Scholars*

THE GREEN BOOK
Writings on Irish Gothic,
Supernatural and Fantastic Literature

edited by
Brian J. Showers

Aimed at a general readership and published twice-yearly, *The Green Book* features commentaries, articles, and reviews on Irish Gothic, Supernatural and Fantastic literature.

Certainly favourites such as Bram Stoker and John Connolly will come to mind, but *The Green Book* also showcases Ireland's other notable fantasists: Fitz-James O'Brien, Charlotte Riddell, Lafcadio Hearn, Rosa Mulholland, J. Sheridan Le Fanu, Cheiro, Harry Clarke, Dorothy Macardle, Lord Dunsany, Elizabeth Bowen, C. S. Lewis, Mervyn Wall, Conor McPherson . . . and many others.

"A welcome addition to the realm of accessible nonfiction about supernatural horror."

– Ellen Datlow

"Eminently readable . . . [an] engaging little journal that treads the path between accessibility and academic depth with real panache."

– Peter Tenant, *Black Static*

REMINISCENCES OF A BACHELOR

Joseph Sheridan Le Fanu

For the first time in over 150 years, "The Watcher", Le Fanu's classic tale of supernatural menace, is reissued from the pages of the *Dublin University Magazine* along with its original companion piece "The Fatal Bride", a brooding gothic novella not reprinted since its first publication in 1848. Like matched duelling pistols, *Reminiscences of a Bachelor* offers the most exquisite balance of craftsmanship, beauty, and peril. In these tales of Old Dublin, honour is ever at stake, the fate of lovers lies mired in the past, and something even worse than deceit stalks the streets, something just as deadly to the soul as it is to the flesh.

"An extremely readable entertainment."

– Wormwood

"Le Fanu's particular gift lay in his ability to be both disturbing and witty about this world, often in the same sentence"

– Supernatural Tales

*"Atmospheric and cleverly built . . .
a suspenseful, enticing narration providing further
evidence of Le Fanu's uncanny storytelling ability"*

– British Fantasy Society

BENDING TO EARTH
Strange Stories by Irish Women

edited by Maria Giakaniki
and Brian J. Showers

Irish women have long produced literature of the gothic, uncanny, and supernatural. *Bending to Earth* draws together twelve such tales. While none of the authors herein were considered primarily writers of fantastical fiction during their lifetimes, they each wandered at some point in their careers into more speculative realms—some only briefly, others for lengthier stays.

Names such as Charlotte Riddell and Rosa Mulholland will already be familiar to aficionados of the eerie, while Katharine Tynan and Clotilde Graves are sure to gain new admirers. From a ghost story in the Swiss Alps to a premonition of death in the West of Ireland to strange rites in a South Pacific jungle, *Bending to Earth* showcases a diverse range of imaginative writing which spans the better part of a century.

> "Bending to Earth *is full of tales of women walled-up in rooms, of vengeful or unforgetting dead wives, of mistreated lovers, of cruel and murderous husbands.*"
>
> – Darryl Jones, *Irish Times*

> "*A surprising, extraordinary anthology featuring twelve uncanny and supernatural stories from the nineteenth century . . . highly recommended, extremely enjoyable.*"
>
> – *British Fantasy Society*